Justice:
the Beginning

Justice #0

SUZAN HARDEN

To Perry

This is a work of fiction. All characters, organizations and events in this novel are products of the author's imagination and are not to be construed as real. Any resemblance to persons, living or dead, is entirely coincidental.

BY SUZAN HARDEN

(Each series is in suggested reading order)

Bloodlines

Blood Magick

Zombie Love

Zombie Confidential

Zombie Wedding

Amish, Vamps & Thieves

Blood Sacrifice

Love, War & a Bulldog

Zombie Goddess

Ravaged

Sacrificed

Reality Bites (Coming Soon)

Ghouls in the Grocery (Coming Soon)

Resurrected (Coming Soon)

Seasons of Magick

Spring

Summer

Autumn

Winter

Justice

Sword and Sorceress 28 ("Justice")

Sword and Sorceress 30 ("Diplomacy in the Dark")

Justice: The Beginning

A Question of Balance

A Modicum of Truth

A Matter of Death (Coming Soon)

A Touch of Mother (Coming Soon)

888-555-HERO

Hero De Facto

Hero Ad Hoc

Hero De Novo

Miscellaneous

Sword and Sorceress 31 ("Pig-Headed")

Sword and Sorceress 32 ("Unexpected")

The Perfect Partner

"Dismissed," Brother Marc said to the room of men. The novice master's gaze focused on me. "Except for you, Luc."

Disbelief punched me in my gut. I hadn't been given an assignment. Did this mean I wouldn't take my final vows later tonight? I almost reached for the gold coin my father had given me when I entered temple service, but I stopped myself.

The money had been his reassurance that if I didn't like it here in Issura, I could go home. Over the years, it had become my good luck charm. But I wasn't about to leave the temple in disgrace. Not when I was so close to finishing my studies.

The other Light novitiates who'd done their two-year stint of the duchy circuits rose and filed out of the room with the orders for their new posts. A few gave me sympathetic looks. The expressions of the rest were a mix of contempt, confusion or pity.

Once the room was empty, I stood. "Brother Marc, may I ask if Justice Clio found fault with my performance?"

He smiled. "Actually, she gave you exceptionally high marks. Come." He beckoned me to follow him.

"Is this because I'm from Cant?" It wouldn't be the first time my commitment or loyalty had been called into question since I hadn't been born in the queendom of Issura.

Brother Marc stopped abruptly, and I nearly ran into him. He stared at me. "Why in the all names of Light would you think that?"

"I-I—" I had acted the fool and spoke before I thought. Just because one idiot from a noble family tried to make my life miserable during my first ten years at the main temple. Or he had until the Lord of Light blessed me with growth in my seventeenth winter.

I inclined my head to the novice master. "I apologize for my rudeness, Brother."

He smiled. "All these years and you're still letting Salvatore get to you." He *tsk*ed and waggled a forefinger before he resumed walking. I rushed to catch up to his rapid strides.

"But I have no assignment—" I tried again.

"The Reverend Father wishes to speak with you."

The Reverend Father? I clenched my fists to keep them from shaking. "Why?"

He chuckled. "He did not share that information with me. He merely asked which of my novices would be best suited for a matter of delicacy. Justice Clio was quite impressed with your empathy and discretion."

Brother Marc said no more despite the numerous questions I peppered him with as we walked through the halls toward the administrative offices of the temple.

We approached the oak doors carved with the twelve-point star inlaid with gold. The wardens who guarded the Reverend Father nodded in acknowledgment. "He's waiting for you, Brother Marc," the one on the right said.

The doors swung open on their own, and I followed the novice master through. The Reverend Father's office wasn't opulent by any means. Plain, polished wood covered everything, including the floors. Brown leather cushioned the chairs. More leather covered the multiple tomes in the bookcases that covered the two side walls. The windows on the opposite wall overlooked the temple's meditation garden.

The Reverend Father sat behind his desk. A fit man despite his sixty-two winters, he exuded an air of quiet determination. He was everything I expected from my glimpses of him over the years. What I hadn't expected was the black-cloaked woman with the milky eyes of the blind sitting across from him.

The Reverend Mother of Balance.

I nearly choked on my saliva.

"Novice Luc as you requested, Reverend Father." Brother Marc bowed. Even worse, he turned and left. The doors closed quietly behind him.

I bowed to the head of our order. "Reverend Father." I had no clue of what was happening, but Papa always said manners never hurt. I bowed to the woman as well though she couldn't see me. "Reverend Mother."

When I straightened, she smiled. "He'll do."

One person stood in the small receiving room at the Temple of Balance when the Reverend Mother and I entered. If the tall, angular woman didn't wear the badge of a justice, I would have thought she was a warden. Her stance suggested action, not thought. She balanced her weight on the balls of her feet, and her hands didn't stray from her sides. If I gambled, I'd lay the one coin I possessed that she carried blades beneath her robes even though she wasn't wearing her temple-issued sword.

Her cowl was pulled so far forward I couldn't discern her face except as a vague shadow. Odder still, I had the distinct impression she could see me from the way her head swept up and down.

"Finally found someone to foist me off on, old woman?" Despite the sneer in her tone, her voice had a husky, sensual quality.

"I had to find an experienced priest of Light who could tolerate your officiousness, my sanctimonious little brat," the Reverend Mother shot back.

By the Twelve, what had I volunteered for out of my ignorance? I'd never heard any of the priesthood, much less a priestess of Balance, snipe at someone the way these two did.

"I'm N—" I stopped myself. After my ordination tonight, I'd be a full priest. I had a strange feeling this justice wouldn't accept anything less. "Brother Luc."

"No. You're not," she said coolly. "Even if I couldn't see your damn novice badge, you just lied to me."

I tested for a truthspell. No magic. Was she lying when she claimed she could view my insignia? That didn't make sense. Only blind women, those touched by the Goddess herself, were admitted into Balance.

The odd justice turned to the Reverend Mother. "You said he was experienced."

"He spent two years in the field, training with Clio, which is far more experience than you have, Anthea."

"You're just sending me out on circuit to scare the villagers."

"Are you disobeying a direct order, Justice?" The Reverend Mother's voice held what could only be described as glee.

Anthea crossed her arms over her chest. "I wouldn't give you the satisfaction."

"Then I suggest you get to know Brother Luc over the next candlemark for he will be a full priest before you leave in the morning." The Reverend Mother pivoted, her black robes flaring out behind her, and she unerringly headed for the black-lacquered door. "Warden!"

Anthea dropped her arms to her sides. "What if I want someone else?" she shouted.

"Then you may stay in this room until you wither up and blow away, my little death wish," the Reverend Mother said over her shoulder. She slammed the door behind her as she exited.

With my hands clasped behind my back, I waited for the justice to unleash her acid tongue at me, but she remained silent. After I counted one hundred heartbeats, I said, "Do you despise Cantish people on principle, or just me in particular?"

"I don't like liars." Her fingers twitched at her sides.

"I didn't realize a handspan of candlemarks so detrimentally affected my rank. I take my final oaths tonight."

Another twitch of her hands. "I . . . apologize for any insult I might have offered you. Novice Luc. Is the Cant Temple of Light so full of priests they send their rejects north?"

Now, she was deliberately acting like a bitch. Maybe the Lord of Light had a reason in subjecting me to Salvatore's taunts in my younger years. If I was forced to spend the next few winters with this woman, we needed to get a few things straight.

I crossed my arms, matching her stance from earlier. "If you're planning to stab me with the knives you have hidden in your robes, please do it now.

I'd prefer an honest weapon through my heart to your constant slights. Lady Justice."

Her whole body jerked. Her reaction surprised me, considering her attitude toward the head of her own order. She forced her hands to relax.

"Then don't ever lie to me again. Or even try to impress me," she said in a more neutral tone.

Agreed, I replied in mind speech.

This time, she literally hopped back a pace. "And stop pretending you want to be here."

"All right," I said mildly. "As long as you stop pretending you want to stay in Standora."

"Stay in the capital?" She sniffed. "Hardly."

"Then what's the problem?"

"Have you been told our assigned circuit? It's the eastern half of the Duchy of Orrin," she said and threw her hands in the air. The movement shifted her cowl back. I caught a hint full lips, medium skin color and a sharp chin before she yanked her hood forward again.

"And?"

"It's Orrin," she growled.

There was far more going on than she would reveal right now. I tried for a conciliatory tone. "We'll be traveling the towns and villages in the foothills. If you insulted the duke or the temple seats in the city of Orrin itself, you won't be anywhere near them."

"What about dispatches and orders?" she grumbled. "Where else are we supposed to—"

"Have you ever actually looked at a map of the region?" I snapped. Justice Clio hadn't been this whiny the two years we traveled together.

"I—" She hugged herself. Whatever she was about to admit, she changed her mind. "No. I've felt one."

Demons take me. Of course, she couldn't see a map. Every priestess of Balance was blind. On the other hand, she'd acted as if she could see me. She claimed she could.

"What about Nastine?" I shrugged. "Granted, they don't have a full-time justice, but Balance maintains a small chapel. It would actually save any messenger a day's ride."

"All right, but there's something else you should know before you chose to ride circuit with me." She brushed back her hood.

Long, black hair cascaded past her shoulders. Her face was as lovely as I'd suspected. But instead of the milky orbs of the rest of her order, Anthea's eyes were blood red.

A day's ride after we left Standora, we turned off the National Road and headed east. Justice Anthea had made it clear within the first league that small talk would not be tolerated. Nor would singing or whistling.

It was nearly first afternoon of a beautiful late spring day when she blurted, "Aren't you going to say anything about them?"

"About what?" I knew what she wanted, but after the difficult time she gave me when we first met, I decided to return the favor.

"My eyes."

"Actually, I'm more interested in why you hate Orrin so much."

I could feel her stare at me.

After a long moment, she said, "You're lying."

"You didn't truthspell me."

Her chin rose. "I don't need a truthspell to know when someone's lying."

"So you can read minds, too." I grinned. She damn well hadn't read mine, and we both knew it.

"It's hard enough to keep everyone out," she murmured. "And I don't like intruding. It feels like I'm violating someone."

That put a new spin on my reticent justice. "I'm sorry for mindspeaking to you the other day. It was not intended as an assault."

"Apology accepted."

Well, that was a start.

I considered her question. Since she thought any type of diplomacy was the equivalent of lying, I decided the truth was my only defense. "I didn't want to violate your privacy, but if you wish to talk about your . . . condition, we can."

She glanced at me as if measuring whether she really wanted to broach this particular subject. "How do they appear to you?"

There seemed to be more to her question than the surface words. "What do you mean? As compared to the rest of your order, or compared to non-members of Balance?"

"Yes, to both questions."

"Haven't you looked in a mirror?"

She toyed with her reins. "I-I can't see reflections."

Now, that was certainly odd, especially since she saddled her horse without assistance. But it did explain the difficulty she had combing and braiding her hair this morning. "And you haven't asked one of your sisters or your temple's wardens or staff about this?"

Her body stiffened. When I didn't think she'd carry the subject further, she said, "The Reverend Mother forbade anyone at Balance from discussing the matter."

Once again, I had the feeling there was more to the story. "Why?"

After another long moment, she sighed. "Because I did this to myself. Could you please answer my original question?"

I almost made a joke about her saying "please" for the first time, but decided against it. If I did, I'd destroy this tenuous connection we had, which would make for a miserable circuit term. It didn't mean I wouldn't take advantage of the situation.

"On one condition."

Outrage filled her voice. "You presume—"

"You haven't even heard my condition yet," I pointed out.

She released the breath she'd drawn for berating me. "All right. What is your condition?"

"You'll let me comb and braid your hair."

"Why?" She sounded genuinely confused.

"Because I'm not riding circuit with a justice who looks like a long-haired cat with mange."

Her hand lifted, but she let it drop. "Agreed."

I hadn't expected such rapid capitulation, so I plunged on before she could reconsider. "The eyes of everyone I've met from your order has a milky or blueish color for the entire orb."

She nodded. "Because we were all born blind, as Balance herself was when she emerged from the darkness of Chaos."

"Yours are constructed as the rest of ours. The main portion is white. But your pupils are blood red. The irises are a shade darker."

She hesitated for a moment before she asked, "And no one else has those colors?"

I blew out a deep breath. "No one I've met. However, sometimes people and animals are born without any color on their bodies. Because there's no body pigment in the way, their blood colors them. I saw a rabbit like that once."

"I believe the term is albino, but I don't look like that, do I?"

I examined her face. Like me, she'd pushed back her hood to enjoy the sun's warmth as our horses climbed the trade road. She really was lovely.

"No. The skin of your face and hands is nearly the same shade as mine, and your hair is black. While I cannot vouch for the rest of you, I would say you're probably not albino."

She inclined her head. "Thank you."

"For what?"

She gave me a sad smile. "For being honest. May I ask a personal question?"

Intrigued by the possibilities, I said, "Yes."

"How do you know how to braid hair?"

I chuckled. "I watched my little two sisters for my parents. It was one of my tasks."

She opened her mouth as if to ask something, but her lips pressed together, and she remained silent.

I didn't realize until we'd made camp that night and she was fast asleep that she'd evaded my question about why she hated Orrin.

The only matters that required temple adjudication in the first two towns on our circuit included a broken fence and a broken inn table. Both involved males who were little too enthusiastic about spring and mating. At least, the farmer with the broken fence got a calf for his trouble.

Ten days into our travels, we camped a half day's ride from our next stop at the village of Mountain Gate. By then, we found it was far better if I made dinner and Anthea cleaned our utensils. Mainly because I was a much better cook.

As she repeatedly emphasized while she wolfed down her food.

I rose and stretched as she scrubbed a tin plate. "I'm going to take a walk."

"You could just say you're taking a piss," she commented dryly.

Apparently, we'd learned each other's habits more than I thought. And for once, my politeness hadn't launched accusations of lying from her.

I bowed to her. "Then please excuse me while I take a piss, Lady Justice."

The corners of her lips twitched. It was the closest to good humor I'd seen from her in our entire trip. After facing away from the fire to let my sight adjust, I strode barefoot into the trees circling our camp.

I had untied my leggings when I heard rustling behind me. Bears, wolves, and panthers were common in the mountainous eastern edge of Issura.

And I'd left my sword and knives with the rest of our gear by the fire.

I slowly turned my head to look over my shoulder.

A polecat stood behind me. An abnormally large polecat. It seemed startled to find me, so it did what polecats do. It twisted its tail toward me.

I ran.

Or I tried to. I forgot I'd unlaced my leggings and I'd left my boots by the fire. A root caught the toes of my left foot. There was a snap that wasn't the root. Sharp pain jabbed through my foot and ankle. I landed hard. If the fall hadn't knocked the air out of my lungs, I wouldn't have sucked in a deep breath full of polecat spray. My aborted shout turned into gagging accompanied by burning, watering eyes.

"Luc?" Anthea called.

I couldn't answer. The need to escape the cloud of noxious fumes was too great. I belly-crawled away, praying to Light the polecat didn't have any family members nearby.

"Luc?"

I looked up. A dark, blurry figure rushed toward me.

"Holy Balance!" Anthea abruptly took several steps back. "You can't blame that smell on the hardtack and jerky."

"It was a polecat."

An odd snorting sound came from the justice. Then a gurgling hiccup. Finally, she laughed so hard she bent over double. I decided she had a nice laugh when she yanked the cactus out of her ass.

Even when her humor came at my expense.

"So glad you find my tribulations amusing." I tried to stand, but another sharp pain shot through my left foot. Several improper Cantish words slipped out before I could clamp my jaw shut.

She sobered immediately. "Broken or sprained?"

"I'm not sure," I forced between clenched teeth.

I couldn't put any weight on my injured foot, so it was a tedious slog back to our camp. Both of our horses whickered and tossed their heads as we passed them.

"Thank you for the assessment, you two," I muttered.

"I have to agree with the horses," Anthea added.

I looked at her. "You can communicate with animals?"

"Don't be an idiot. I would have been transferred to the Wilding Temple if I had that kind of talent," she said as she lowered me to the log by our fire to sit. "Now, take off your clothes."

My pulse jumped, and other parts of me were about to make a very improper show through my untied leggings. "Excuse me?"

She'd already knelt beside me. Thankfully, her sole focus was on my injury. Her fingers gently probed my foot.

"I'm no healer, but your little toe is definitely broken, and I think you may have torn some ligaments as well. We need cold water, and you can't leave on your leathers in case there's more swelling overnight. Do you have—"

She looked up and her mouth formed a perfect 'O'.

I'd assumed the stench of the polecat spray would have calmed my physical reaction to her touch. I was wrong, so I waited to see what she'd do next.

Anthea's mouth closed and her lips tightened. Finally, she said, "I see your foot and your uniform aren't the only things that need a dip in a mountain stream. Do you have some civilian clothing?"

"Bottom of my left pack, there's some wool trousers."

She rose and strode to where my gear lay. Well, she wasn't screaming imprecations at me for a totally involuntary reaction. However, nothing like this had happened with Justice Clio. But then she hadn't been as . . . enticing.

"I beg your pardon?" Red eyes glared at me across the fire.

Between my broken toe and the distraction of her touching me, I'd forgotten she had a talent for mindspeech. I'd have to be more careful about stray thoughts. "There's packet of pain powder in the right bag," I said.

Her mouth opened and closed, but she dropped the subject.

Once she retrieved the items, we hobbled down to the nearby stream. Anthea's sense of direction was unerring. Neither of us stumbled or tripped though there was no true path. She settled me on a large rock. The water flowed swiftly from the snow still melting higher in the mountains. I dipped in my foot, and blessed cold numbed the pain.

"Shirt," she demanded.

I stripped off the silk. The effort left my eyes burning from my wildlife encounter coating the material and my skin prickling from the cold.

She clicked her tongue as she took the offending garment between her thumb and forefinger. "We're going to need apple vinegar to remove the smell. Unless you happen to know a spell?" She placed the shirt in the stream and set a stone on it to keep it from floating away.

"I was hoping you did." I wiggled on the rock and managed to remove my leggings. Thank Light, no moon shone to embarrass me further. Matters had devolved during the trip to the stream, but now they were reasserting themselves.

"No. And I don't think a veiling spell would help." She quieted as she mixed the powder in one of the cups she'd just cleaned. "Was there anything odd about the polecat that sprayed you?" she asked when she handed me the cup.

"Other than its impeccable timing?" I said sourly.

"Yes."

I downed the bitter concoction as I considered her question. A little wine would had gone a long way in alleviating the nasty aftertaste of pain powder. I handed the cup back to her. "It did seem unusually large."

She took the cup and handed me a waxy bar. I sniffed it. The odor of olive oil mixed with something floral.

"It's Aleppo soap. It won't remove all the polecat odor, but the soap should tame it enough so the horses and I don't have to find another campsite." She snatched my tainted leggings. "Call for me when you're done." She scurried off through the undergrowth.

Now how had she seen my leggings in the dark? She wasn't blind like her sisters, but there was something definitely different about her. Intriguing.

I glared at my own body. "Down, boy."

I rinsed the soap from my body and hair, but the night had become too cold to stay in the stream or let everything dry naturally. After struggling to pull on wool over damp skin without aggravating the broken bones further and wringing out my shirt, I called for Anthea.

Nothing.

I shouted again.

Nothing.

I resorted to mindspeech. *Anthea!*

For the love of Balance, you don't have to scream in my head. An edge of worry underlaid her mental chiding.

What's wrong?

I don't think you encountered a polecat.

Really? I definitely smell like someone who did.

I'm well aware of that fact.

Someone crashed through the underbrush further upstream than our camp and it came in my direction. My muscles tensed. *Please tell me that's you making the racket.*

A predator would be a little more quiet. Once again, a dark figure rounded a tree and approached me. Nor did the figure look like a woman in the dark.

"Yes, it's me," Anthea snapped. She glanced back in the direction she came. "Did you sense any magic when you ran into the polecat?"

Maybe she'd accidentally given me more pain powder than I thought because she wasn't making sense. "I was a little more concerned with getting away from the creature before it sprayed me. What do you mean magic?"

"I went back to the spot of your encounter. There was—" She shook her head. "I'm not sure. You're injured, and we're both tired."

We retrieved our belongings and headed back to our campsite. Between the icy stream and the powder, the pain in my foot had subsided to a dull ache, but I still needed her assistance navigating through the woods.

She swore when we entered the clearing. Clothing and equipment lay scattered across the dirt surrounding our fire. Someone had gone through our belongings.

"This mess wasn't caused by wildlife," I said.

"Sit down. I'll clean up. If I get my hands on the little bastards who did this—"

My prickly justice was back.

Guilt tugged at my conscience as I sat on the same damn log while she sorted our gear. She was kind enough to pile my belongings next to me so I could repack my own saddlebags.

More improper Cantish fell from my lips as I realized what was missing. Not just my purse, but the gold piece Father had given me as well. And it had been hidden in a secret pocket of my dagger sheath.

"What?" She looked up from where she was folding her spare clothing.

"My stipend is gone. And a gift from my father."

My statement sent her searching through her own things. "My stipend, too." She slapped her saddlebag. "That little bastard!"

"What?"

"The shapeshifter that sprayed you."

"What?" I asked again.

"He or she waited until one of us went to relieve ourselves. They sprayed. While we dealt with the mess, they or their companion robbed us."

I frowned. "You're jumping to conclusions." I looked around our camp-site. "However, it wasn't bandits. Our horses and swords are still here."

"And we would have *heard* them." She tapped her temple, then huffed as she returned to folding her spare robes. "It had to have been someone local. We're three days from the next nearest town to Mountain Gate. Temple weapons or new horses would attract too much attention, but coins wouldn't be questioned."

The gold piece taken would be questioned, but I didn't feel like dealing with Anthea's barbed tongue. In the fortnight I'd known her, I'd learned one thing. She'd want to know why I bothered to keep something from my life outside the temples.

"If you're right, our little thief is also talented," I said. "That still doesn't answer why they stole from clergy."

"We'll find out," she muttered. "Even if we have to truthspell every single person in Mountain Gate."

I swallowed my groan. I had no doubt she'd do everything in her power to do exactly that.

We rode into Mountain Gate shortly after first afternoon. The smaller children rushed to greet us and were immediately repelled by the lingering odor of the polecat.

Since the tiny village didn't sport an inn, we rode to the equally tiny chapel in the village square. The middle-aged priestess of Mother who rushed out to greet us staggered back a couple of steps, and her face contorted.

"Oh, my." She covered her nose and mouth with her hands.

"I apologize for our odiferous introduction, Mother. I'm Justice Anthea," my partner said. "My colleague, Brother Luc, had an unfortunate encounter with some local fauna last night."

"So I noticed," came the priestesses muffled reply. "I'm Mother Margaret." She waved toward the rear of the chapel with one hand. The other hand remained firmly clamped over her nose. "There's a tub at the back. Lucky for you, it was wash day so I have water heated already."

"Could I trouble you for some apple vinegar as well?" Anthea asked.

Mother Margaret shook her head. "I don't have enough for a big, strapping fellow like the brother here. But I have a barrel of wine vinegar that'll do the trick. Vinegar and scoop of natron will leave you smelling like yourself again."

"That may not be an improvement after all," Anthea replied. Despite her sharp words, an impression of lightness came from her. Was she trying to make a joke?

Margaret smiled at me. Or I think she did. Her hand over her nose also covered most of her mouth. She waved for me to follow her.

I limped behind the mother as she led me to the tub while Anthea took care of the horses. "She does quite well for a justice, doesn't she?"

I grinned. "I wouldn't mention it to her if I were you. She can be rather cantankerous."

"Really?"

"Ever wake a bear during hibernation?"

The priestess laughed. "Understood."

Mother Margaret gave me a hollow tube of carved wood to breathe through since my entire body needed to be submersed in her wine vinegar concoction. Apparently, I wasn't the first person in Mountain Gate who had an encounter with the abnormally large polecat.

My attempts at meditation while soaking failed. The figure of a certain justice stalked through my thoughts with her dark, straight hair and her barely-there smile.

Anthea's prickly psyche brushed against mine, and I quickly shut away my improper thoughts. I had taken my oaths to my order two weeks ago. Why was I thinking about her in that way now?

The softer, gentler aura of Mother Margaret accompanied the justice's. One of the women tapped on my wooden tube. I raised my head out of the warm fluid and wiped the stinging vinegar out of my eyes.

"I think you've sufficiently soaked, Brother," Mother Margaret said.

Anthea cocked her head. "You smell much better."

"I feel like a grape," I muttered.

"Would you like me to stomp on you?"

Mother Margaret's eyes widened at Anthea's comment. However, I wasn't quite sure if she were joking or not either. Not after certain things that had happened last night.

"I have enough broken bones, thank you. I'll pass for now," I answered. I carefully climbed out and wrapped my lower half in the towel the mother offered.

"You could go back to Emerald View," Mother Margaret said. "They have a journeyman healer."

"By the time we got there, he have to break and reset the bone." I gave her a rueful smile. "That would put us a good six days behind schedule just in travel time."

Anthea deliberately kept her attention on Margaret while the older woman drained the tub into the village's sewer system. "Speaking of which, are there any disputes awaiting us?"

"None that have been filed, Justice," she said over the gurgling vinegar. "Mountain Gate is a quiet village." She hesitated. "However, there's been some odd occurrences . . ."

"You mean thefts," I said.

Margaret jerked, then grudgingly nodded. "'Twere little things at first. A tart cooling on the windowsill. A hunk of cheese from a cottage while the family was out herding livestock. But the frequency has been increasing." She pursed her lips and shook her head. "The latest was the night 'fore last. Swift Foot—he's a trapper and hunter. Well, he commissioned a new skinning knife from Andrew the blacksmith, and the blade disappeared from the forge. And Andrew is registered. Someone deactivated his alarm spell."

Anthea frowned. "So much for my theory."

Margaret glanced at me. "Which was?" The last of the wine vinegar drained from the tub and she quickly rinsed it before she gestured for me to climb back in.

"That the culprit was someone local and untrained." I dropped my towel before I settled in the tub. "She's leaving out the part where she thinks the thief was a shape-shifting polecat." I grinned at the justice, which earned me an ugly scowl. And not just for teasing her about her theory.

I shrugged. "It still may be someone local—" The pitcher of warm water Margaret dumped over my head cut off my words. I wiped the water from my eyes before I continued. "A common knife is still safer for our thief to carry than a temple-forged blade."

"Temple-forged blade?" Margaret's attention switched from me to Anthea and back. "What the demon are you talking about?"

"We were robbed last night while we were at the stream dealing with our unfortunate situation," I admitted.

"Your unfortunate situation," Anthea said sourly.

"You two were robbed?" Margaret's eyes widened.

"Yes, we were relieved of our stipends." Irritation burbled to the surface now that the polecat smell wasn't clogging my mental functions. "Whoever it was also took a gift from my father. They can have the coins but I want . . ." An idea burst through my annoyance with the thief.

Anthea cocked her head. "What are you thinking?"

"A tracking spell. The gift has been in my possession since my seventh winter. Surely, some of my power has penetrated the metal over time."

Anthea shook her head. "A tracking spell can only be used on living matter."

More water splashed over my head courtesy of the mother.

I spit and swiped the excess from my face. "What about thirteen winters' worth of skin flakes and oils." I held up my hands and rubbed my thumbs over my fingers.

Anthea shook her head, disgust evident on her beautiful face. "I hope you take better care of your sword while I ride circuit with you."

"I *always* take care of my sword." I grinned at the justice.

Mother Margaret took advantage of my distraction to dump more water over my head.

Once I was deodorized enough to converse with respectable villagers and my foot wrapped to stabilize the injury, I dressed in my spare uniform before Anthea and I visited Mountain Gate's blacksmith. She decided a bit more information was necessary before I cast the tracking spell. Luckily, his customer who'd commissioned the stolen knife was at the smith's forge as well.

"Ne'er seen the like o' it," Andrew said between blows of his hammer. He stood a half a head shorter than me. Dense red hair covered his thickly muscled arms, making up for the lack of it on his head. "Weren't even a hint of magic left. Like someone ate it."

"Is there anyone in the area who also has talent?" Anthea asked.

Swift Foot shook his head. "Other than Mother Margaret, just the two of us are registered."

"So there might be unregistered talents running loose?"

The two men stiffened at her implication.

In my most placating voice, I said, "Please forgive the justice. She didn't sleep well after a disturbance at our camp."

Swift Foot relaxed, and he chuckled. "Everyone in a league's radius could smell your disturbance, Brother."

"Which brings me to my next question," I rushed to say before the justice insulted them further. "Has anyone reported an unusually large polecat in the area?"

The two men exchanged looks, and the blacksmith paused in his hammering.

"Yeah." Andrew finally nodded. "At a handful of the farms."

Anthea opened her mouth.

Don't say a word, I ordered. From the anger radiating around her, I would be paying for that statement later. "In conjunction to the thefts?" I asked aloud.

"Only four times with the farms and the polecat. All of those incidents happened the summer 'fore last." Andrew picked up the piece he worked on and shoved the cooling metal back into the furnace. "Last summer, 'twere mainly travelers like you two."

Swift Foot nodded. "I've tried to track the creature three times. As Andrew said, the magic disappears." He waved a hand. "Just gone."

"What material did you use for your spell?" Anthea actually sounded curious.

"Fur caught in the bushes and a fence post the first two times," Swift Foot said. "The last time was a broken toenail in the camp of a Master Weaver from Eagle Ridge who was passing through."

She turned to me. "Your plan might work if the shapeshifter can only shield itself and not the items it or its compatriots steal."

"So little faith, Lady Justice?" I grinned.

"I'll have more if your backward tracking spell works."

In the end, we waited until the next morning to try my admittedly insane idea. I didn't want to break anymore bones, stumbling around in the dark. Mother Margaret found a larger boot in her donation box. She rewrapped my foot and ankle, using a thick pad of rags along the sole to keep my bones from moving.

"This is never going to heal at all if you don't stay of it, Brother," she said.

"Can't be helped this time." I carefully pulled on the larger boot. The sensation reminded me of when I was a boy, attempting to walk in my father's shoes.

After we broke our fasts, Swift Foot joined us at the chapel. "So how exactly is this reverse spell of yours going to work?"

It felt very odd to be the instructor. I also didn't want this attempt to fail in front of the justice.

And why did I care so much about Anthea's opinion? It was more than avoiding her tart tongue. I'd never worried about making a mistake in front of Justice Clio.

A basic tracking spell found the rest of the whole from a few bits. I fine-tuned the magic by weaving the leather mold of the coin with my fingerprints on the gold. The ribbon of energy sputtered until I tied my name and my father's into the spell. Deep gold light hovered above the trail into the forest behind the chapel.

Swift Foot whistled in appreciation. "They didn't teach that trick at the training school for talents."

Anthea snorted. "Let's see what we find before we congratulate the brother." She stalked off to mount her horse.

When Swift Foot glanced at me, humor with a touch of sympathy emanated from him though his countenance remained impassive. Only a cheek muscle twitched to betray his feelings. He was smart enough to keep silent.

Apparently, I hadn't made things as clear between the justice and myself as I thought before we started our circuit. However, this wasn't the time or place to confront her. The hunter and I climbed on our horses and followed Anthea up the trail.

The tracking spell turned off the trail and headed deeper into the forest.

At this elevation, the rocky outcroppings interspersed between the trees were a danger to the horses.

Swift Foot frowned. "That's the direction of Hiram's cabin."

"Who's Hiram?" I asked as I dismounted.

"He was our village cobbler until his wife Sarah died in childbirth ten winters ago."

Anthea rounded her horse to join us. "You definitely need to get a healer for your village."

"Sarah was our healer," Swift Foot replied. Bitterness and pain filled his tone.

Now, I understood why the Reverend Mother wanted me to accompany Justice Anthea. She needed someone to pull her feet out of her mouth.

"He is still grieving?" I asked.

Swift Foot ignored the justice and focused on me. "As far as we know. Mother Margaret and a few women would come up here with food for the child until she died three winters ago. After that, Hiram started shooting at anyone who comes near. Mother Margaret even managed to get the High Brother of Death from Orrin to visit, and he got an arrow through his shoulder for his trouble."

The justice stepped between me and Swift Foot. "Did anyone see the child's body?"

"Anthea!" I spluttered. The hunter looked equally flabbergasted.

"Did anyone else see her body?" she said again. "Or at the very least, her ashes?" She flipped back her hood and glared at the man.

"I-I do not believe so," he said.

She turned to me. "We've found our shapeshifter."

I crossed my arms. "What makes you think that?"

"How old were you when you first showed signs of talent?" She whirled to face Swift Foot again. "Or you."

The hunter and I stared at each other. Finally, he nodded. "The age would be right for an early bloomer."

I cocked my head as I regarded Anthea. "It doesn't make sense. Why would he hide her?"

"Think about it." She laid a hand on my arm. "He's already lost his wife. If Mother Margaret found out his daughter had talent, she'd send the girl to a temple for testing. Hiram might never have seen the child again. He couldn't take the chance of losing her. She's his last link to his wife."

I wasn't sure what amazed me more. That the justice was touching me when it wasn't absolutely necessary, or that she actually had some empathy for the grieving widower.

"So why are they stealing?" I asked.

She shrugged and removed her hand. "It sounds like the girl may be planning to run away given the items she's taken recently."

"Stay here with the horses while Swift Foot and I follow the tracking spell."

"Pardon me?" my prickly justice exclaimed.

It was my turn to shrug. "If you're correct, the girl might try to steal one of the horses while we deal with Hiram. She may listen to you as opposed to another man when her only experience is with her father."

"That's . . . logical," she conceded finally.

"Logic *is* a required course for our temple, too. Not just yours."

One of her black eyebrows rose. "Indeed? Good to know you excel in something besides cooking and talking."

A scathing retort was on the tip of my tongue, but I held back. For some strange reason, I suspected she was as discomfited by her touching me as I was. Instead, I tapped my temple. "Call if you see either of them."

The tracking spell led to an ancient gnarled oak, the kind that one normally didn't see at this elevation. A ridge of granite cupped its roots and kept the tart soil of the pines from leaching into its space.

Swift Foot and I looked at each before we stared up into the branches again.

"You might as well climb down. We know you're up there," I yelled.

A pale face with riotous brown curls popped from behind new leaves. "Go away before my father shoots you." It disappeared into the foliage.

Swift Foot turned to scan the surrounding area. There were too many places an archer could hide up here.

I chuckled. "I'm more afraid of you spraying me again than your father shooting me."

The girl's face appeared again. "Go away."

"What's your name?" I asked.

"Reby." She looked at the gold ribbon. I no longer had any doubts about Anthea's theory if the child could see it. Reby was one of us.

"Greetings, Reby. I'm Brother Luc." When she didn't hide again, I continued. "I'd like to speak with your father about some items that have disappeared around Mountain Gate."

"My father didn't take nuthin'!" Anger twisted her mouth.

"I know he didn't," I said calmly. "But I think he might be able to help me retrieve them from the tree."

She climbed down far enough I could make out her raggedy clothing and unkempt nails. "You're lying."

"Do you know what a truthspell is?"

She nodded.

"There's a justice not far from here. You can ask her to truthspell me. That way you know I'm not lying."

Her gaze flicked toward Swift Foot before it settled on me again. "You're here to take me away to the temples." Her chin lifted. "Like my father always said."

I inhaled and slowly released the air from my lungs. What I said next could make all the difference in a peaceful resolution to this problem. "Actually, I came up here because I want my gold coin back. It was the last present my father gave me before I entered the Lord of Light's service. The rest of our money is yours, but may I please have that coin back?"

Only her eyes moved, flicking between me and Swift Foot. "If I give it back to you, will you leave my father alone?"

"If that's what your father wants."

"That's what he says." She blinked rapidly to keep her sudden tears from falling. "It's not what he needs."

"Is that why you were collecting things?" I asked gently. "To help him?"

"No." She gulped. "I—"

"You want to leave?"

"He won't even let me visit Mountain Gate." She kicked angrily at some leaves. "He says Mother Margaret will take me away if she finds out—" Fear replace irritation on her face.

"That you can change shape?" I said. "I hate to tell you, but quite a few people already know. Or don't you remember spraying me the night before last?"

"I, um . . ." She kicked at the same poor leaves again.

"Do you know why you couldn't disrupt my tracking spell like you could Aaron's alarm?"

She shook her head.

"Do you want to know?"

She nodded.

"Then come down. Let's find your father, and discuss a proper education for you."

"Just a moment." Reby disappeared from sight, but from somewhere above me came the distinctive sound of metal on metal.

She reappeared with a bag slung over her shoulder. The golden end of my spell was firmly attached to her sack. She scrambled down the trunk nearly as fast as a squirrel.

"You're the first polecat I've ever met who can climb a tree." I winked at her.

She giggled and handed me the bag. From the heft, she'd amassed more than anyone realized. Retrieving my father's coin, I dissipated the tracking spell when I felt the tickle of Anthea's mind.

Luc. I found Hiram. Or rather he found me and the horses. She sounded faintly amused. Reby's eyes widened, and I realized she could hear the justice, too.

Are you all right?

For now, but I suggest you back come soon. I don't like the way he's shaking. Especially with a knife this close to my throat.

We jogged back to the clearing where we left the justice and our horses. Reby had no problem keeping up with two grown men and didn't complain a step. The girl was far more mature than I expected for someone with such quick fingers and lack of manners.

Anthea sat on a small boulder near the picketed horses. As she reported, Hiram held a knife beneath her jaw. Like his daughter, he was lean and muscled, but his clothing were filthy rags.

"Reby! Come here!" he snapped.

The girl sucked in a harsh breath and clutched at my cloak. The scent of polecat filled the air. Sharp energy grated along my nerves, the familiar prelude to a Wildling shifting their shape.

I looked down at the girl. "It's all right, Reby." I turned back to her father and injected at much calm into my voice as I could. "Why are you threatening a priestess, Hiram? A justice at that?"

"Give me back mah daughter!"

I held up my hands. "I haven't taken Reby anywhere, Hiram. She's right here. We encountered her on our way to visit you."

"Give her back, or I'll kill the witch!" Bright scarlet drops beaded along Anthea's skin, but she held perfectly still and remained uncharacteristically quiet. I prayed she hadn't misplaced her trust in me to resolve this situation.

"She's blind, Hiram. Are you really going to slit the throat of a helpless woman who hasn't laid a hand on you?" Anthea's irritation at my choice of words brushed against my psyche, but thank Light, she held her tongue.

He glanced down at the justice. "I don't have a choice. I can't let you take mah girl." His tone carried an enormous amount of grief.

"And how are you going to stop me, Father?" Reby stepped from behind me. "You can't watch me all the time. You have no idea what I want. And keeping me with you ain't gonna to bring Mother back."

"You're the only thing I have left of her." Hiram's whole body shook, not just his arm. He would accidentally slit the justice's throat if his tremors didn't halt. She was smart enough not to gloat that she had correctly guessed his motives.

Swift Foot took a step closer. Like me, he held out his empty hands. "No one wants to separate you and Reby, but she needs to learn how to control her talents before she accidentally hurts herself or someone else." He took another step closer. "Please, Hiram. You know Sarah wouldn't want you or Reby to suffer alone up here."

"How would you know what she'd want?" Hiram spat.

"She was a kind and caring woman. She'd never harm anyone or anything. And she saved my life." Swift Foot nodded toward Anthea. "What would she say if she saw you right now?"

"She—" Hiram swallowed hard. "I—" The knife dropped a finger length.

Anthea threw her body backward, her arm shoving Hiram's wrist up and away from her throat. She crashed into him, and they went down hard. Her somersault ended with Hiram disarmed, her boot firmly planted on his sternum, and her sword point digging into his own neck.

I wasn't sure if his wheezing breaths came from getting the air knocked out of him or more likely, his first good look at Anthea's eyes.

"Father!" Reby shrieked.

I grabbed the girl. Her body shivered under my grip. "Don't make things worse," I whispered in her ear.

Anthea glared at the man beneath her foot. "If you ever lay a hand or a weapon on another person again, I will separate your head from your body. Do you understand?"

"Yes," he said.

Without taking her eyes from her prisoner, she asked, "Did you find your father's present?"

For a moment, I questioned what she would do to Reby if I told the truth. The girl had stolen from more than one person, and the law was clear on the matter. I settled for a simple "Yes."

Anthea blew out a sharp breath. "Hiram, if I have your word you will not cause us anymore trouble, I'll release you."

"You have it." Panic tainted his voice. "Just, please, take my hand. Not hers. Have mercy on my daughter, Justice."

So he had a clue of what his daughter had been doing after all.

Anthea made a disgusted sound in her throat. "Maybe if you hadn't been a fool raising her, she wouldn't be such an idiot." But she removed her foot from his chest, sheathed her sword, and held out her hand.

He took her aid and climbed to his feet. However, he was smart enough not to run. Instead, he knelt, bowed his head, and rested his arm on the boulder. "Do it."

"Oh, for the love of Balance! Stand up," she snapped. "No one's cutting off anything today. I'm not compounding your multitude of mistakes with one of my own."

Reby ran to her father. They clung to each other, both of them saying over and over again how sorry they were.

Surprised at Anthea's decision, I kept my mouth shut in case my prickly justice changed her mind about cutting off body parts.

Once we returned to Mountain Gate, we first visited Andrew the blacksmith. Reby had dumped the skinning knife, without the protection of a sheath, into the bag of coins. Anthea arranged for the child to clean out the ashes from the forge for a week while Andrew repaired the blade.

The justice took out our stipends from the stolen funds. From the remainder, she paid Swift Foot to escort the father and daughter to Orrin, Reby for testing at the Wildling God's Temple and Hiram for emotional care at the Child's. The rest she quietly gave to Mother Margaret for tending anyone who needed aid.

Anthea also made a point of taking a lock of hair from both Hiram and Reby. She pointed out the penalties for their actions were severe. If they failed to arrive in Orrin, she'd know, and she would hunt them down. Not even I doubted her on that count.

Despite the padding and the extra-large boot, my left foot ached by the time we settled Hiram and Reby at Mother Margaret's chapel for the evening. With the pleasant night and lack of additional beds in the chapel, Anthea and I camped by the outdoor hearth the priestess used for heating water.

"I can't believe you didn't sense Hiram approaching you," I said as I unwrapped the bandages.

"I did." She sipped the tea Mother Margaret had brought to the justice before the priestess retired to bed.

"Then why didn't you stop him from using you as a hostage?"

She shrugged. "Because I could have taken him at any time."

I threw up my arms in exasperation. "It looked like you were just going to let him cut your throat!"

"Now why would I do something as idiotic as that?"

I snorted. "That's what I'd like to know. Because I'm wondering if the Reverend Mother of Balance is right about you having a death wish."

"I don't," she muttered, staring into her cup.

I didn't have to truthspell her to know she was lying. What had happened to her that left her so scarred? Maybe I needed a different tactic.

"Are you ever going to tell me why you despise Orrin so much?"

"Maybe." She sipped her tea. "Someday."

I lay down, using my saddle as a pillow, and watched the stars. Her answer only made me more determined to chip away at the granite wall she'd built around her heart.

And that's when I knew I was in really deep trouble.

Courting Trouble

Shi Hua ducked under the punch aimed at her face. Her right leg shot out and swept her opponent's overbalanced one. Reverend Father Chen landed on his torso with a loud *WHOOF!*

She pounced, one foot on the back of his neck and her bamboo stick at his throat. "Yield."

"Excuse me, Novice?" A hint of anger vibrated in the priest's words. The crowd tittered. Whether due to the Reverend Father of Conflict's ignominious defeat at the hands of a Light Novice, or her lack of etiquette, she wasn't sure.

However, her face heated at the rebuke. But it didn't mean she would grant an opponent any mercy even in a festival tournament. "Yield, Reverend Father."

"I . . . yield," he ground out.

A gong sounded, and the crowd erupted in cheers and whistles. She removed both her foot and her stick from the Reverend Father's person and held out her palm. He ignored her hand and struggled to his feet, which only added to the laughter of the spectators.

Under the sound of the crowd, he muttered, "I'll enjoy having the impertinence beat out of you, girl." He stomped out of the fighting ring, not even bothering to brush the copious dust from his tunic. He hadn't even bowed to her as custom and etiquette demanded.

She stared at his retreating back as her win was announced.

Shi Hua still sat in the bathing quarters when the bells of the temple rang first evening. She fingered the jade bracelet that had been the prize for top place in the Spring Rituals martial arts tournament. Maybe beating the

Reverend Father of Conflict hadn't been such a good idea after all. Maybe she should have found a way to gracefully lose.

"I was wondering where you'd gotten to." Brother Lin, the Light novice master, shuffled across the dressing area and plunked his hefty girth on the bench. The wood creaked beneath his mass. He nudged her bare shoulder with his elbow. "Still upset Chen was rude to you?"

She sucked in a deep breath. "I don't think me studying at the Temple of Conflict is such a good idea, Brother."

"Oh, ho! So you think you already know everything about the martial arts because you won a trinket?"

She stared at him in horror. "I don't think that! I swear by the Twelve!"

"Well, that's a relief." He smiled. Whenever he did, and he did often, he reminded her of the giant statue of Light himself in the main sanctuary, his benevolent expression always reassuring.

Usually, Brother Lin's smile was infectious, but today's worry didn't prompt a return smile from her. "It's just . . . you told me to do my best. And I did. Now, Reverend Father Chen hates me."

"Hate is a very strong word. Nor is it a synonym for 'embarrassed'."

Shi Hua scowled at the novice master. "I didn't mean to make a fool of him."

"No." Brother Lin chuckled. "He did that quite ably on his own by underestimating a girl of fourteen winters. He's lucky bamboo sticks are substituted for live steel in the Spring Rituals games."

She slumped against the tiled wall behind her and looked at the ceiling. "I don't understand why I'm being sent there for additional lessons."

"For the answer to that, you would have to ask someone more knowledgeable than myself. Our own Reverend Father doesn't share everything with me, my child. He merely asked me to recommend a female student with certain qualifications.

"For now—" He took her hand and placed five silver coins in her palm. "Since you earned a decent sum for me by knocking Chen on his face, go have some fun with your friends." He waggled a finger to indicate her state of undress. "But please, put some clothes on first. While you haven't taken your final vows yet, a pregnancy would not reflect well on me as your master."

The nighttime celebrations were in full swing by the time she ventured out of the novice quarters. Paper lanterns were strung between buildings, and firecrackers popped everywhere. The Grand Plaza was packed. She pushed through the throng. Several people started to say something rude until her uniform registered. It was one of the good things about belonging to the temples.

She finally found the tables in front of the Ministry of Husbandry. Sure enough, fellow novices Jian, Mei Wen, and Fa waited there for her.

"Sorry I'm late." She plopped down next to Mei Wen, and Fa pushed a cup of chilled hibiscus tea into her hands.

"I can't believe you kicked the ass of a reverend father," he said. The brittle energy along Shi Hua's nerves said he was barely keeping his shapeshifting in check with the festival's excitement.

"May I feel your bracelet?" Mei Wen asked.

"Of course." Shi Hua pulled it off her wrist and placed it in her friend's waiting hands. Most people gave the clergy of Balance a wide berth, even the novices. When Mei Wen refused to keep her hood up as most of her sisterhood did to hide their milky orbs, Shi Hua knew they'd be great friends.

"Trouble at home?" Jian asked.

"Not per se, but Brother Lin is gambling again."

Jian winced. "What is it this time? Chariot racing? Archery? Dice?"

She pulled a silver piece from her belt. "Me. The next round is on him."

Once they finish their tea, they walked around the merchant booths set up along the Grand Plaza's perimeter. Shi Hua kept a tight grip on Mei Wen while they walked. And as the four friends had for the last five years, they headed back to the Temple of Balance well before the empress's annual address.

Since the sisterhood of Balance couldn't see the fireworks display, and most of their staff was at the Grand Plaza or elsewhere, no one stopped them from going up to the roof and watching the finale of the evening.

Shi Hua clasped Mei Wen's hand so her friend could see the display through her eyes. Magic tingled along her skin, not just from Mei Wen, but also from the court sorcerers even though they were several blocks away.

"That's odd." Mei Wen cocked her head. "I don't hear the empress."

"Crown Prince Chengwu is giving the address tonight." Fa said. "I heard through a friend at Death the empress is very ill."

Jian shrugged. "For every life, there is a death."

"It doesn't mean death should come sooner than it is meant to," Shi Hua chided.

"If she dies, how will things be different?" Mei Wen asked. "Jing will continue as it always has."

For some reason, this discussion bothered Shi Hua, but she couldn't put a finger on why. Her questions faded when a cheer rose from the plaza.

The noise vibrated through the stone of the temple, and the first fireworks exploded in the sky. The lights formed into the figures of Empress Bao De and her armies in the final battle against the demons for the heart, soul, and life of Jing over a century ago.

Every child in the land knew the story. The empress ordered the priests and priestesses of the Temple of Light to unleash their magic on the demons even though she and her consort were in the way as they held back the tide. A blinding white explosion finished the show, just as the magic had finished both the demons and the empress. Blue embers trailed down from the sky, a reminder of Jing's grief that their empress had sacrificed herself to save her people.

Mei Wen sighed. "Thank you. I so love that story."

Shi Hua released her friend's hand before Mei Wen could *hear* her own fears. That she would be required to sacrifice herself for the accidental insult she had inflicted on Reverend Father Chen.

———◇———

Seven days later, Shi Hua reported to the Temple of Conflict's novice master. He examined her papers, looked her up and down, and made a sound of disgust. "Not here, idiot girl. Go to the Reverend Father's office."

She turned to go when the novice master yelled, "And tell Lin I'm spreading the rumor he cheated!"

Shi Hua swallowed a grin, pivoted and said, "Yes, sir!" before she marched out of the training room.

The instant she was out of the novice master's sight, she ran for the administrative offices, which unfortunately were on the opposite side of the complex. Sweat dripped in her eyes as she slid to a halt well short of the double doors carved with the crossed axes and inlayed with iron, indicating the office of the Reverend Father. No sense getting her head chopped off by his personal wardens over a misunderstanding.

"Novice . . . Shi Hua . . . of Light . . . I have . . . an . . . audience," she managed between huffing breaths.

"You're late," the one on the left complained. The two wardens shared a look. "She's the reason I lost a gold coin," he told his partner.

"She's the reason I could afford the dowry for my betrothed." The one on her right looked at her and winked. "Wipe your face before you go in," he whispered.

She grabbed the hem of her cloak and did as he suggested.

"And don't show fear," he added. "Reverend Father Chen eats terror for breakfast."

Not trusting her voice, she nodded.

He opened the door. "Novice Shi Hua of Light, reporting for training," he called out.

She marched in as confidently as she could. The door clicked shut behind her. Before the chief priest's desk, she bowed. "Reverend Father."

"Don't they teach novices manners at Light anymore," he snapped. "A novice should always recognize her betters!"

She hurriedly straightened and looked around the room. Off to the side, two other people sat. The man wore the soft gray of Thief with the badge of the head of the temple.

She gulped and bowed again. "Reverend Father."

The woman wore the scarlet veil and robes of Love, but Shi Hua recognized the twinkling cinnamon eyes. "Aunt Yin Li!"

"That's Sister Yin Li to you, Novice! I swear to Conflict, this child has no discipline." Reverend Father Chen lowered his face to his hands and groaned.

Yin Li rose, and Shi Hua launched herself into her aunt's arms. Between her studies and her aunt's duties they hadn't been able to speak much recently.

When Yin Li pulled away from their fierce hug, she said, "As glad as I am to see you, my niece, Reverend Father Chen is correct regarding your manners." She smiled. "Or lack thereof."

Shi Hua stepped back. "Please forgive my lapse in etiquette, Sister." She executed an appropriate bow. "It shall not happen again."

Yin Li turned to Reverend Father Chen. "May I suggest Brother Shang for Novice Shi Hua's Conflict teacher since you seem to have taken ill?"

Chen lifted his head and glared at Shi Hua. She bit her inner lower lip to keep from reacting to his furious expression.

"That would be a very good idea, Sister," he growled.

The Reverend Father of Thief rose from his chair. "Then we shall take our leave of you, Chen. We have no wish to keep you from your duties." He crooked his finger to indicate Shi Hua should follow him.

Once outside of Reverend Father Chen's office and away from the wardens, the Reverend Father of Thief said, "I am Biming."

Shi Hua swallowed hard. The clergy of Thief never gave their names. For someone of his stature to give her his public name meant he either trusted her completely. Or he planned to kill her.

She bowed. "Thank you, Reverend Father."

"Come then." He pivoted and marched down the corridor. She had to jog to keep up with his long strides and Yin Li's gliding steps. He made so many turns through the halls of Conflict, Shi Hua was thoroughly lost. The sounds of fighting echoed down one corridor, and she was relieved when he slowed and entered one of the doors without nasty crashes behind it.

She followed Yin Li through to find herself in a massive arena. It was easily twice the size of the public arena used for the martial arts tournament during the Spring Rituals. Below the spectator benches, two sets of twenty priests faced each other on the sand. Both genders wore only blood red loincloths and were armed with staffs. A yellow flag was planted behind one group, a blue flag behind the other.

A single man, dressed in the boiled red leather and brass link armor of the Temple of Conflict, stood on a platform on the opposite side of the arena. She had the distinct impression he was aware of everyone in his domain, including her.

"Shi Hua!" Yin Li hissed. Her aunt motioned her to join the two senior clergy on a wooden bench.

As she gingerly sat, the dressed Conflict priest called, "Begin!"

War cries rang out before the two groups charged each other. The scene devolved into what appeared to be chaos. She soon noticed a pattern. Not just a pattern, but a violent dance with its own movements.

The first two ranks of each group were the primary attackers, their focus solely on the opposing team's flag. The last two ranks defended their respective flags. If one of the attackers knocked down an opposing defender, then an opposing attacker fell back and took the defender's place.

Finally, the yellow team had no attackers left. The blue team had two, and try as they might, they could not penetrate the wall of yellow defenders.

One of the blue defenders took advantage of the opposing team's concentration. Retreating to her team's flag, she ran towards the yellow team. She thrust her staff into the sand, vaulted over the heads of the fighters, and snatched their flag off its pole as she landed.

Her compatriots erupted into cheers. The yellow team's members looked dumbfounded until an angry expression covered one girl's face.

She marched closer to the platform. "Brother Shang, I protest! That was an unfair maneuver!" Several of her compatriots voiced their agreement.

The slight rise of the priest's eyebrows silenced everyone. "What have I said about using that word in my classes?"

Her shoulders slumped. She bowed to the priest. "Forgive me, Brother Shang. I spoke without thinking."

"We will discuss individual and group performances tomorrow. After you have a chance to cool down and look at such objectively." His gaze swept across his students. Again, Shi Hua would have sworn his attention included her. "For now, you are dismissed."

His students replaced their staffs in an equipment rack and left the arena in clumps of three and four. The girl who had captured the flag and the girl who protested bent their heads close, whispering as they pointedly looked at Shi Hua. Their attention didn't seem malicious, but it unnerved her nonetheless.

Once all the students had left, Reverend Father Biming crooked his finger again. "Come, ladies."

They met the Conflict priest near the steps into the arena floor. After the Reverend Father made the appropriate introductions, Brother Shang appraised Shi Hua. "So you are my special project?"

She blinked and tried to maintain her composure. "I am unaware whether I am a project to be completed, sir."

Yin Li tittered, and a wide grin spread across the Reverend Father's face.

"Ah, dissembling as well. I see why Brother Lin suggested you."

"With all due respect, Brother, but suggested me for what? He would not tell me."

Brother Shang folded his arms over his chest. "He could not tell you because he does not know."

"She should not know until her training is complete," Reverend Father Biming said.

Shang chuckled and shook his head. "Thieves and lovers so enjoy their secrets, don't they, my little Light novice?"

She had the distinct impression that the flood waters of the Yellow River were about to close over her head. "I would not know, Brother. Light is all about exposing the truth of matters."

He cocked his head. "You don't think both truth and secrets are necessary, Novice?"

"Yes, they are, Brother. However, the use of each depends on the circumstances."

His eyes twinkled though the humor did not reach the rest of his face. "Very good, Novice. As a reward, I will give you one truth. You were chosen because you are a distance speaker. However, Brother Lin was unsure of your range. Do you know?"

She shot a desperate look at Yin Li.

Her aunt inclined her head to the Conflict priest. "Brother Shang did you the courtesy of giving you a truth, my niece."

Shi Hua sucked in a deep breath. "I spoke with Sister Yin Li often from our farm outside of Yintze, Brother."

A shocked expression appeared on the Reverend Father's face. "All the way from southern Chu?"

Brother Shang merely nodded as if he expected such information.

"We knew she had mind speech from the time she was born," Yin Li added. "But when she spoke to me after I arrived here in Chengzhou to begin my training . . ."

Shi Hua stared at the toes of her uniform boots. It was always the same when adults found out what she could do. They treated her gift like it was some marvelous thing, or they found her an oddity. Both attitudes made her feel as if she should be in a zoo.

"We're not putting you in a zoo, Novice," Reverend Father Biming said.

Fear itched along her spine.

"Nor do you have anything to fear," he added. "And no, I am not reading your mind. I have a touch of empathy, but not enough to divert me to the Temple of the Child."

Brother Shang nodded, almost as if to himself. "Let's see what I have to work with. Take off your robes, Novice. Sister, if you would do the honors." He turned and started down the stairs.

Shi Hua quickly untied her temple robes and removed them. Hopefully, she wouldn't sweat too much in her silk shirt and leather uniform leggings. She endured enough scolding from the chief laundress at her home temple.

Yin Li's veil and robes jingled from their multitude of bells as she removed them. Underneath, she wore a form-fitting half shirt of stiffened scarlet silk and short trousers of the same material. She kicked off her sandals and followed Shang to the sand.

Since the brother hadn't said anything about removing her boots, Shi Hua left them on and bounced down the stairs.

Brother Shang tossed her a staff. "Now, if you can knock your aunt over as you did my reverend father during the tournament finals, I will be truly impressed."

She looked at the wood in her hand, then back to the priest. "But that's hardly fair! I'm armed. She isn't."

His mien grew quite stern. "I will not expect more from you than I do my Conflict students, but were you not here when another young woman complained about fairness?"

"Yes, sir."

"If I give certain parameters in a lesson, then I expect you to honor and obey them. However, in battle, you must learn that an opponent will take advantage of your weaknesses. Therefore, you must do the same to them."

She bowed to him. "Yes, sir."

This should be far easier than fighting Reverend Father Chen. And that simple thought worried her. She turned and bowed to Aunt Yin Li.

And received a face full of sand as a result. Apparently, honor was not today's lesson.

Half-blinded, Shi Hua raised her staff in both hands out of instinct. She barely blocked a spinning kick that would have knocked her on her backside.

Sweet, lovely Aunt Yin Li gave her no quarter. She alternated punches and kicks so fast that Shi Hua had to retreat. Another spinning kick cracked her staff in half.

Well, Brother Shang hadn't said they couldn't use talents or magic.

Shi Hua dropped the broken fragments of the staff. She dived under a back strike aimed at her head, rolled and launched a light ball in her aunt's face when she whirled to resume her offensive.

Yin Li staggered back, momentarily blinded. Shi Hua rushed her aunt, but Yin Li managed to sidestep the attack. She summoned a piece of the broken staff to her hand. When Shi Hua flew past, a cracking blow landed on her buttocks. Like Reverend Father Chen during the tournament, she landed chest first on the sand.

The embarrassment was worse than the actual hit on her backside. Her lungs ached from the lack of air, but she knew she wouldn't be given an ounce of leniency. She scrambled to her feet and circled her aunt, trying to catch her breath and think of some way to end this at the same time.

Brother Shang didn't say she couldn't obtain another staff either. Yin Li must have reached the same conclusion. She rushed at Shi Hua with a wild cry.

Shi Hua whirled, snatched another staff, and knocked over the rack for good measure. She backpedaled to gain some distance.

Yin Li danced back to avoid the falling wood, but a handful of staffs hit her toes and feet. The other half of the broken staff flew to her left hand. She limped while she kept pace with Shi Hua's circling, watching her through narrowed eyes.

Shi Hua chewed her bottom lip. How in the Twelve was she going to finish this without harming Yin Li or getting herself seriously injured in the process?

Her aunt twirled the broken ends as if they were batons. She darted forward. Shi Hua responded. With two quick cracks of her staff, she knocked the wood from Yin Li's hands.

Instead of retreating, her aunt slipped inside the range of the staff, knocked it away, and simply shoved. Shi Hua tried to backpedal, but Yin Li's legs tangled with hers. She fell on her back, knocking the wind out of her once again.

Yin Li's knees landed on her upper arms. Her elbow pressed against Shi Hua's throat, hard enough to be painful.

Not quite hard enough to crush her windpipe.

A nasty smile twisted Yin Li's lips. "Yield."

Shi Hua stared at her opponent. It was like she didn't know her aunt at all. "I . . . yield," she choked out.

Yin Li climbed gracefully to her feet and held out her hand. Her face transformed back to the sweet, lovely girl who had watched Shi Hua as a child.

She took her aunt's hand and pulled herself upright.

"The girl has potential," Brother Shang pronounced.

"Good," Reverend Father Biming said. "For now, Novice, you will attend your Light classes in the morning, combat lessons with Brother Shang in the afternoon, and instruction from Sister Yin Li in the evening."

Shi Hua opened her mouth, but the Reverend Father held up his hand. "Your first lesson from me is how to keep your silence without the need for me to place you under a compulsion spell. You are not to mention these lessons to anyone. You are not to ask questions." He smiled. "Yet, anyway. When Shang and Yin Li tell me you are ready, then you will start seeing me for additional instruction."

She fidgeted. She told her friends everything, as they told her their secrets. It didn't seem right doing something without knowing why, but the Reverend Father of Light wanted someone with her talent for this project, and Brother Lin had recommended her. The idea of disappointing Brother Lin warred with her loyalty to her friends.

In the end, the need to uncover the truth concerning this special training won out over her other emotions. She bowed. "I understand and agree, Reverend Father."

"Very well." He inclined his head to Brother Shang. "She is yours for the rest of this morning and afternoon."

Yin Li hugged her. "Ask for me when you come to the Temple of Love after the evening meal."

"Yes, Sister." She bowed to her aunt.

Shi Hua turned expectantly to Brother Shang as the other two clergy left.

He frowned. "Your staff work was sloppy. Let us focus on that today. But first, right the equipment stand you knocked over and replace the weapons.

"Yes, sir." She bowed and started on her tasks.

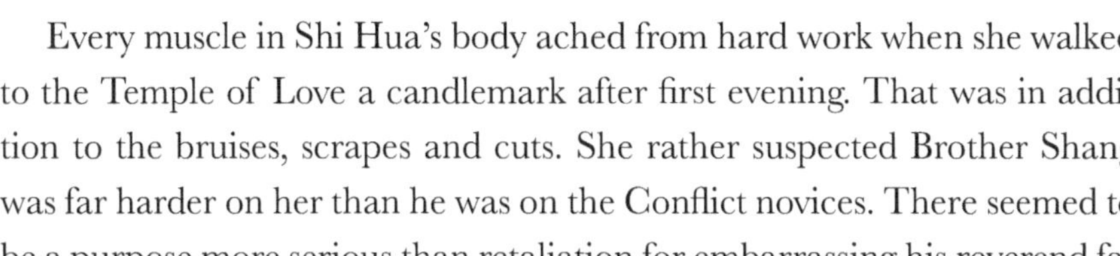

Every muscle in Shi Hua's body ached from hard work when she walked to the Temple of Love a candlemark after first evening. That was in addition to the bruises, scrapes and cuts. She rather suspected Brother Shang was far harder on her than he was on the Conflict novices. There seemed to be a purpose more serious than retaliation for embarrassing his reverend father, but she'd assured Reverend Father Biming she wouldn't ask questions, so she kept her mouth shut.

Jian had tried to ask her about the Conflict training over the evening meal. She shoveled dinner into her mouth in an effort to discourage him. Finally, she said, "Reverend Father Chen's making my life miserable over losing the Spring Rituals tournament, but he's not going to make me quit." Considering the black eye she sported, Jian took her at her word and said nothing more.

However, the two wardens at the doors of the Temple of Love frowned at her when she approached them.

She straightened her back and said, "Light Novice Shi Hua to see Sister Yin Li."

"What is this pertaining?" one of them asked.

There wasn't a doubt in her mind they would have driven her away if she hadn't worn her temple uniform. She jutted out her chin. "I was instructed to relay the message from the Reverend Father only to her."

"Very well," the other warden said. "I'll escort you. We don't want any of the worshippers inside to think you're a novelty for them to enjoy." He opened the door and strode inside.

She wanted to breathe a sigh of relief they didn't question her half-truth. When she crossed the threshold, the sights in the reception room left her shocked. Growing up on a farm, copulation wasn't a foreign concept, but the sheer robes the sisters wore left nothing to the imagination. And the behavior of those worshippers waiting for a private room! She focused on the back of the warden while she followed him.

The laughter and jingling bells faded. The warden reached a plain, varnished door and knocked. When no one answered, he opened the door. "You can wait here."

She entered the utilitarian bedchamber, but instead of leaving, the warden entered behind her, closed the door, and locked it.

"Take off you clothes," he ordered as he unbuckled his scarlet quilted jacket.

Her heart hammering, Shi Hua reached for her power as well as the knife inside her cloak. Aches were forgotten as she tensed. With no windows, the warden stood between her and the only exit.

He tossed the jacket on the bed. "You really can't tell?" The voice was no longer male, but a very familiar female's. She laughed.

Shi Hua cocked her head. "Aunt Yin Li?" She stared harder at the person across from her to verify what her ears said. "You scared the piss out of me!" She sheathed her knife.

"Language, child." Her aunt continued stripping off the warden uniform. "And scaring you serves you right for dumping that rack on me this morning. I'm lucky none of my bones were broken." Yin Li stopped and shot her a pointed look. "And your manners are still lacking, Novice."

"I beg forgiveness, Sister." Shi Hua bowed. "Do I need to disrobe? Or was that part of your act?"

"Yes, remove your clothes. You need to be aware of your body for tonight's lesson."

She did as she was instructed. Nudity hadn't bothered her before. Part of the discipline within the Temple of Light was to control natural desires and not let them control her, but here in the Temple of Love, her lack of clothes gave her a sense of unease.

"Our first lesson will deal with the differences in how men and women move." An equally naked Yin Li sat in front of her dressing table, pulled out a cosmetics chest, and removed an ointment jar. "But first I need to get off this Goddess-cursed beard. The glue itches like you would not believe."

She opened the jar and selected a brush from her chest. "How did I move differently this evening than I did this morning?"

Shi Hua thought for a moment. "When you walk in your Love robes, you take smaller steps as if you were crossing ice." She grinned. "At least until you stepped onto the sand. Tonight, your strides were longer, more . . . aggressive."

Yin Li's reflection smiled at her from the polished brass mirror. "That's a good start. Why didn't you trust me when I first told you to remove your clothes?" She stroked the ointment gently around the edges of her false beard and moustache.

"B-because I didn't know it was you. I thought you were going to . . ."

Her aunt turned and stared into Shi Hua's eyes. "*Always* question everything. But you need to learn when to voice those questions aloud, when to remain silent and watch, when to fight, and when to run." She peeled off a bit of the fake hair and brushed on more ointment. "You'll quickly discern when a situation can turn ugly."

Something else wasn't quite right about her aunt's deception. "May I ask a question now, Sister? About your disguise?"

Yin Li chuckled. "Yes, you may."

"How did you transform yourself so thoroughly? When I started to summon a light ball, I felt no other magic in the room. You did not use a glamour."

"Part of it was my dress. Part of the deception was your own preconception. You've lived in a temple since you were seven, therefore you automatically trust all wardens, correct?"

Shi Hua nodded.

Yin Li peeled off the last of the beard. "But when you had visual confirmation of the services we provide worshippers, you assumed the same would be expected of you."

"You made a comment about me being mistaken as a treat."

"And that unnerved you further, so your concern was for your safety from a worshipper, not any possible danger I presented until it was too late." Yin Li took out a larger ointment jar and started spreading the cream over the reddened areas of her cheeks and chin. "Could Empress Bao Yu afford such a luxury of trusting all of her guards?"

"Of course she should . . ." Shi Hua's shoulders sagged as one of Brother Lin's recent lessons crystalized in her mind. "But the familiarity of her staff puts her at a disadvantage. One of them may harbor resentment for a slight, real or imagined. Or a political opponent may play a far longer game than the empress realizes. Therefore, no, she cannot afford to trust anyone, much less her guards."

Yin Li rubbed the remnants of her face cream on her hands into her elbows. "Who is more dangerous to the imperial family? The schools of philosophy or the temples?"

Shi Hua opened her mouth, and realized the trap of the question. "Both are equally dangerous to the imperial family, but the abilities of each side keep the other in check. The nobility is far more dangerous than either the schools or the temples since they have the most to gain should anything happen to the empress or the princes."

Another realization hit her. "It is true then. The empress is dying."

Yin Li ignored her question and rose from her dressing table. The non-answer was confirmation unto itself. "As I said, you will learn to move like a man tonight."

Shi Hua collapsed in her bed as the temple bells tolled first night. She expected exhaustion to claim her, but too many questions ran through her mind.

The familiar presence of Mei Wen entered her mind. *Shi Hua?*

Yes.

Is everything all right? You feel troubled.

It was so tempting to spill everything, but she had promised Reverend Father Biming. *Like I said last week, Reverend Chen was not happy about the results of the tournament, and I am paying for it.* She rolled over trying desperately to find a comfortable position. The pain powder Brother Lin had left for her in her room only took the edge off her aches from her lessons.

I overheard some of the justices today. Fa was right about the empress. They don't expect her to live through the Vintner's Festival.

It's nothing for us to worry about. She's old. The crown prince is young and healthy, as is his older brother should something happen before he sires a child.

Fa says the brothers and sisters at Wildling are worried, too.

Shi Hua rolled to her other side. She didn't want to admit the Wilding priests' behavior was unusual. They rarely worried about anything. *I'm sure they are all nervous about any possible change. The empress has sat on the Dragon Throne for nearly fifty years. People have a tendency to get set in their ways.*

Fa says the seniors are worried the Prince Consort has too much influence on his son. It's no secret that the Prince Consort believes the demons are no longer a threat, and there's no reason for the temples.

Can we talk about this later, Mei Wen? I'm exhausted.

Of course. Good eventide.

Unfortunately, Shi Hua was still awake when the bells tolled second night. Mei Wen's comments mixed with the unspoken truths of her new instructors. Something was about to happen, and the temples were preparing for it. But by the Twelve, why would they put their hopes in a fourteen-year-old novice?

The next month passed in a crazy blur. Shi Hua's extra lessons at Conflict and Love were held everyday, even on Rest Day. Whatever event that worried the seniors, they were determined to prepare her before it happened.

Jian and Fa were perturbed she no longer spent free time with them. Mei Wen merely asked every night if everything was okay.

And she couldn't tell them a damn thing.

At the end of the first month, Yin Li said, "This is our last evening. Tomorrow night will be your first lesson with the Reverend Father of Thief."

Shi Hua's heart sank. The time with her aunt had been the one thing getting her through these extra lessons.

Yin Li cupped Shi Hua's chin and tilted her head up. "Do not fret so, my niece. I've taught you all I can." She laughed. "Everything except the arts of bedplay."

"They don't expect me to . . ."

"No, child. They will honor your vows." Yin Li cocked her head. "Are you having second thoughts about remaining with the Temple of Light?"

Shi Hua shook her head. "The only thing that bothers me about all this is—" She sucked in a deep breath. "My friends hate me because I'm not spending time with them, and I can't tell them why."

"Oh, child." Yin Li pulled her close. "You are all at the age where you'll be separated soon due to your duties. You just happen to be the first."

She swallowed hard. "Do I go to the Temple of Thief tomorrow evening?"

Yin Li's smile was odd, and for the first time in Shi Hua's memory, it did not meet her eyes. "He will come to you."

The next day after Conflict training, Shi Hua returned to her quarters from the bathing room. A package sat on her bed. She set aside the basket with her grooming accessories.

Examining the cloth and twine-wrapped parcel from several angles, she came to the conclusion she was as paranoid as the senior clergy. She untied and opened it. Black-dyed cotton spilled out along with a note: *Put these on after the evening meal. Nap if you can. It will be a long night.*

The note wasn't signed, but the sender was obvious. Now, how had the Reverend Father Biming slipped into the Temple of Light, much less the novice quarters, without being seen?

Shi Hua asked him as much when he appeared in her room at first night.

He chuckled. "Did you not learn anything about disguises from your aunt? Come now." He checked the hallway before he exited her room.

She followed. The novice section was noisier than she realized. Fellow students snored or stirred in their sleep. There was the faint thump of boots from wardens making their rounds. And behind her came the *shoosh* of bare feet on wood.

"Sneaking out? That's a switch. You're usually sneaking in at this time of night."

She whirled to face Jian. "Go back to bed," she hissed.

"I'm not a tattler, but so help me, Shi Hua, you'd better tell me what's going on, or I'll fetch Brother Lin." Anger and hurt emanated from him.

She glanced around, but Reverend Father Biming was nowhere to be seen. "Go back to bed, Jian."

"No." Though he wasn't much more than a shadow in the dark corridor, the crossing of his arms was obvious. "Not until you tell me what's going on."

How did she convince her friend without breaking her promise to Reverend Father Biming? "Have you been listening to Fa?"

Jian snorted. "Please. It's bad enough he's got Mei Wen wrapped up in knots with his conspiracy . . ."

She stepped forward and laid a hand on his shoulder. "Listen to me. I need your help. Keep your eyes and ears open around here. Tell me if anything unusual happens."

"How can I when you're never here?" he asked sullenly.

"We'll meet in my room every day after the evening meal. Just us. Don't tell anyone else for everyone's sake. Please, Jian, this is more important than you realize."

He cocked his head, but his shoulder relaxed under her hand. "Fine, but I expect the truth at some point."

Shi Hua breathed a little sigh of relief when he patted her hand and headed back to his room. Since the Reverend Father was no where to be seen, she headed in his original direction, down the corridor toward the gardens.

"You handled that much better than I expected," came a low voice behind her as she opened the gate.

She jumped, pivoted and drew her knife all in one motion.

Reverend Father Biming chuckled under his breath. He passed her and plunged through the foliage, not taking one of the stone paths.

She winced. The gardener would be furious in the morning if he saw any bruising on the plant leaves, but she trailed Biming anyway. When they emerged from the greenery, a rope hung from the top of the outer wall of the complex.

The Reverend Father clicked his tongue. "I really need to speak with Jin about the laxity of his wardens." He turned to Shi Hua. "Can you climb this?"

"Yes, sir," she whispered and scrambled to the top. A month ago, she wouldn't have been able to. Was that part of the reason Brother Shang emphasized working on her upper body strength?

Biming climbed up behind her. At the top, he straddled the wall, pulled up the rope, and flung it over the other side. He had Shi Hua climb down to the alley. "Catch," he softly called.

She managed to catch the climbing hook so it didn't clatter on the brick pavement and alert the wardens. To her amazement, Biming pushed off as if to jump, but floated down from the top of the wall instead.

Remembering her promise not to ask questions, she handed him the climbing hook and coiled rope. He placed them in the bag slung over his shoulder.

He started walking, sticking to the back alleyways. "Do you know what I'll be teaching you?"

She matched his strides. "While I would not presume to say for sure, I can guess, sir."

"Very well." He grinned. "Your first lesson is sneaking into Brother Shang's quarters and retrieving a bag of coins."

She gulped. If she had any belief her extra lessons would start to get easier, it withered under her daunting task.

When Shi Hua arrived for her Conflict lesson the next afternoon, Brother Shang said nothing, simply held out his hand. She dropped the small purse in his outstretched palm.

He opened the pouch and counted the coins before he looked up at her. "Good to know you haven't lowered yourself to Thief's lesser aspects."

Shi Hua gritted her teeth to keep from making an impertinent remark about him ridiculing her honor.

Brother Shang chuckled. "Good. You're learning not to react to an insult. I wish more of my students could learn that lesson. We will discontinue our classes on Rest Day, though the other six days you will still report here in the afternoon."

She blinked. "But Brother—" The disappointment that flooded her was a surprise.

"Yes, Novice?"

He didn't brook any backtalk, and she realized she was about to do just that.

She lowered her head. "I beg forgiveness for speaking out of turn."

"Permission to speak freely, Novice."

The tears filming her vision were as much a surprise as her disappointment. "I will miss your training sessions, sir."

His smile was almost tender. "We're not quite done yet, Novice." He produced three silver coins from his purse and set them on the ledge of the practice arena. "They're yours if your arrows can hit the bullseye ten times in succession."

She blinked away the wetness, grinned and reached for an unstrung bow.

Spending the afternoon of a Rest Day with her friends turned into a slightly difficult task that required the use of one of her silver pieces to purchase bribes of sweets and jasmine tea. They retreated to Jian's room to talk and eat.

"The brothers and sisters here are worried, too," he said after eating his third lemon cookie. "I was cleaning sconces in the main sanctuary and accidentally overheard—"

"Eavesdropped, you mean," Mei Wen teased.

Jian shrugged. "Whatever. But temple seats from the provinces are sending in word there's talk of the princes clashing over the throne."

"Why?" Fa said around a mouthful of bamboo tart. "The succession is clear."

Mei Wen frowned. "Legally, yes. But that doesn't account for the human desire for power. Are you allowed to say anything, Shi Hua?"

She shook her head. "You're assuming I've been told what's going on. All I can say is it's not just our respective temples who are worried. They all are. Except . . . I don't think it's about the succession."

Jian reached for another lemon cookie. "Any time there's a shift in power, there are those opportunists who try to seize it during the transition."

Shi Hua shrugged. "All we can do is the same thing the senior clergy are doing. Wait and see."

For the next month, a pall hung over the capital. Shi Hua's lessons with Reverend Father Biming were her only relief, mainly because of the entertainment factor of disguising herself and, well, stealing things and putting them back.

After taking and returning the dies for stamping currency, she and Biming sat on the roof of the Ministry of the Treasury, munching on figs, when the temple bells started ringing. When they didn't stop and the bells from every other facility joined in, she knew.

Empress Bao Yu was dead.

Lessons were halted for all the novices, including her special instructions with Brother Shang and Reverend Father Biming, as all the temples dealt with the increase in citizens looking for comfort.

Unsure of what to do since her entire day wasn't scheduled for the first time in ages, Shi Hua sat with her friends on the steps of the Temple of Balance. They watched the influx of nobles and other important personages arrive in the capital. Imperial guardsmen were every few yards to keep people from interfering with the traffic, except for the section of the road dominated by the temples.

Fa kept a running description of the carriages, litters, and chariots passing by for Mei Wen, but his attempts at jokes fell flat.

The bells had started tolling first evening when Shi Hua spotted the man across the wide thoroughfare. He was dressed as middling merchant, but his attention darted between the Balance wardens and those of Light across the way. His pockets bulged with round objects, and she spotted the disguised sheaths of throwing knives. The deep shadow of the Temple of Balance and twilight helped mask his odd behavior from most observers.

She followed his gaze down the street. A litter in imperial red with the sigil of the crown prince came toward them, the carriers jogging at a rapid clip. She scanned the street and spotted three more men and a woman acting as peculiarly as the one across from her. She muttered a prayer for her special teachers and their excellent lessons. The five people planned to pincer the litter.

With the wardens stationed at the temple doors and on the rooftops, they wouldn't get to the litter on time. And if she called out to the wardens, assuming they listened to her, the five assassins would disappear into the crowd.

Mei Wen nudged her. *What's wrong?*

Shi Hua clasped her friend's hand and showed her what she saw. *How good are you at mind control?*

One, maybe two at best.

Take the two down by Thief. Hold them until the wardens can get to them, "Fa. Jian. Follow me.

"Huh? What?" Fa looked around wildly, but Jian grabbed his arm and dragged him along.

"Two men ahead," Shi Hua muttered to the boys. "One on the steps of Mother. The other standing by the nearest lamppost of Father. I'll take the one at Light. Be careful. The Reverend Father will need one of them to truthspell."

Fa immediately turned serious as he realized what was happening. "Got it." He split from Jian and headed for the Temple of Father.

"You'd better be right," Jian muttered back.

She ignored him and focused on her target. Panic threatened as she realized the litter would reach the assassin before she'd get to him.

The disguised merchant reached into his pocket, took out an object and threw it at the front contingent of carriers.

The flash bang detonated the instant Shi Hua recognized it. She ran and dove for the curtains of the falling litter.

And prayed to Light as she flew through the air the surrounding guards wouldn't kill her before she got the crown prince clear of his transport.

She crashed into the man inside. Her momentum carried them through the curtains on the opposing side. They landed on top of the assassin with a loud *crack!*

The disguised killer screamed as hands yanked her off the crown prince. The horde of people shouting deafened her. Her lungs burned from the acrid smoke of the flash bang.

Her voice added to the cacophony as she was dragged away. "Assassins! Protect the crown prince!"

"Shi Hua. Stop," someone hissed in her ear. She looked up to see Brother Lin and Reverend Father Biming with firm grips on her arms.

Once she stopped resisting, Biming said, "Take her to her quarters. I'll gather the other three."

Brother Lin continued dragging her up the steps of Light. "What the demon were you thinking, girl?"

He charged through the doors and toward the novice quarters. Rage was the only description for the look on his face. In all her years at the temple, she'd never seen him angry. She shivered. Whatever punishment he or the Reverend Father meted out didn't matter.

"Is the crown prince all right?" she asked timidly.

Brother Lin paused and glanced at her. "I don't know, child." He resumed his march to her room without releasing her. "I don't know."

Shi Hua paced in her tiny room until Brother Lin unsealed the area and fetched her. Relief swept through her when the novice master unsealed Ji-an's door as well. Her friend had scratches on his face, but otherwise seemed unharmed.

I'm sorry, she said silently.

He shrugged. *Lashes will be the worst that happens. They can't get too mad since we saved the crown prince and apprehended the assassins.*

She hoped he was right, but that little positivity was dashed when they were escorted across the street to Balance. All twelve of the temple heads sat in the courtroom there as well as the novice masters for Balance and Wildling.

Shi Hua's worry for Mei Wen and Fa was assuaged when she spotted them sitting on a bench next to the Reverend Mother of Balance. They appeared far more intact than Jian or herself.

Brother Lin led her and Jian to the same bench and pointed. They quickly sat.

"Now, would you four like to explain what happened in front of my temple two candlemarks ago?" the hooded woman in black asked.

Shi Hua jumped to her feet and bowed. "It was all my fault, Reverend Mother."

"Really?" she said dryly. "You hired the assassins to kill the crown prince?"

"N-no, m'lady."

"They should have alerted the wardens!" Reverend Father Chen shouted. "They should be punished!"

"For what? Saving the crown prince? Or is this your ego talking?" the Reverend Mother of Balance snapped.

"It's definitely his ego," the Reverend Mother of Child chimed in.

The heads of the other temples snickered or laughed outright.

This is a farce forced by Chen. They know exactly what happened. Shi Hua wasn't sure if she should be relieved or concerned about that realization. But if Chen needed a pigeon to sacrifice . . .

She cleared her throat. "May I have permission to speak, Reverend Mother?"

"Yes, you may."

Even though Shi Hua couldn't see the priestess's face, she had the impression the head of the Temple of Balance wasn't angry at her.

"I'm the one who egged on the other novices. It was my idea to act, not theirs. I willingly accept sole punishment for our transgression."

"And I will gladly mete out her punishment," Reverend Father Chen snarled.

"You will not touch one of my novices without my leave," the Reverend Father of Light said mildly. "As it is, both of my novices will be reassigned to keep them away from you."

Shi Hua's heart sank to her knees. And Jian would hate her for the rest of their lives.

Shi Hua trudged into her room. Brother Lin said he would speak to her after he was done with Jian. She wasn't looking forward to yet another reprimand for the evening's adventure.

She closed the door to find Reverend Father Biming standing behind it.

He smiled and held a finger to his lips. "Change," he whispered and pointed at a bundle on her bed.

She did as she was told. This time, he had given her the gray uniform of a novice from his own temple.

As he had the first night of their lessons together, he surreptitiously checked the hallway before leading her silently to the temple compound's wall. She no longer needed a rope, having located all the finger and toeholds of this portion.

This time they ran and leapt from wall to roof and back again across the city. She hesitated when she realized their destination.

"After the excitement of earlier, the Imperial Guard will be extra alert," she whispered.

"By the Twelve, I hope so," Biming exclaimed. He levitated to the ground while she climbed down after him.

With no buildings to aid them or trees to shield them, how would they enter the palace? After the assassination attempt, marching up to the gate and asking for admittance apparently was out of the question. Biming led her north.

Ahead, the white arches of the aqueduct flowing into the Imperial Palace shone in the moonlight. She sighed. It could have been worse. He could have led her in through the sewers.

"Not when you're meeting with the crown prince," Biming whispered. "Now keep your mouth and your thoughts quiet."

She did as she was told while they climbed the aqueduct. The water entered through a hole in the palace's outer wall that not even a toddler could squeeze through.

He placed both hands on the bricks and murmured a spell. The tiny entrance yawed large enough they could duck inside. He whispered another spell, and the opening shrank to its original size.

In the absolute darkness, Shi Hua started to form a light ball.

Biming slapped her hand. "The court sorcerers will know."

The sharp *snap* of steel on flint sounded before a lantern flared to life. He led her down a winding staircase and through what she suspected were hidden corridors. Again, she was thoroughly confused by all the twists and turns. Without Biming, she'd never find her way out again.

Finally, he paused and peered through an eyehole. He pressed a brick and a door opened.

Shi Hua blinked against the blinding brightness of a multitude of lamps. A hooded man in Imperial red sat on a raised dais.

Biming dropped to his knees on the bamboo floor mat and bowed low. She swallowed hard and quickly followed his example. There was only one person in all of Jing who received such respect.

"Light Novice Shi Hua as you requested," the Reverend Father of Thief murmured.

"Your Imperial Majesty," she said.

"How do you feel about saving someone who's not the emperor?" the man said.

Despite protocol, her head jerked up. He pushed back his hood.

The new emperor's brother, Prince Po, sat on the dais.

Shi Hua wasn't sure what to expect when the prince dismissed Reverend Father Biming and they were alone. He waved for her to sit at the low table close to the dais. A steaming pot and cups sat on the surface.

"Thank you for saving my life tonight," the prince said.

"Your life?" She blinked.

He chuckled. "I guess you were too busy landing on top of me to see who you were saving."

Her face heated. Of course. With his mother's death, he became the crown prince until his brother sired an heir. "You are most welcome, Your Highness" she said, bowing again.

"Enough with the bowing." He gestured sharply. "And the titles. I get too much of that lately by people who don't mean it."

The secret door rattled. She half-expected the Reverend Father, but the man who stepped through resembled Prince Po too much to be anyone else but the emperor.

She immediately rose to her knees and bowed again, her forehead touching the bamboo mat.

"Didn't you tell her there will be none of this nonsense during our meeting, Po?"

"Of course, I did, brother."

"If this is Biming's idea of his best and brightest, Jing is in a lot of trouble," the emperor said sourly. "Sit up, girl!"

She obeyed, and was further shocked when both men joined her at the low table. Prince Po began pouring the tea.

"You may speak freely here. I'm sure you have many questions about the reasons for your unusual training," the emperor said.

"I'm terribly confused, Your Imperial Majesty," Shi Hua said.

The emperor looked at his brother, who glared at her in turn.

"I'm sorry, but it, I mean, it's not, well . . ."

"The matter is simple," Prince Po started. "My usefulness to my brother in Jing is coming to an end." He handed her a steaming cup of tea before his brother, which did nothing to calm her nerves. "While he is well aware of my loyalty to him, others are not so sure. Or they wish to replace my supposed influence with their own." The emperor gave an amused snort, but Prince Po ignored him. "The purpose of your lessons was to be my bodyguard."

"Me?" she squeaked. "Surely, there are others who are bigger, better skilled at magic—"

"I will be leaving Chengzhou shortly after our mother's funeral and my brother's coronation," Prince Po said. "I will need someone who knows how to pass unnoticed."

She nodded. "That's the reason you need a distance speaker, to stay in contact with your brother. But people will notice you being gone, especially since . . . oh!"

The emperor nodded. "The impending birth of my new heir will be announced once Po is safely out of the city."

"That doesn't explain why you need someone from the temples, sir," she said.

"I cannot trust any of the schools of philosophy for reasons I will explain to you when we are safely out of Jing," Prince Po said.

"No one beyond the three of us, your own reverend father, and Biming will know about this," the emperor added. "You will not tell your friends or family. To everyone else's knowledge and belief, you and a team of Light wardens will be assigned to a trade convoy en route to Shang La. All of you will allegedly be killed in a landslide to my everlasting grief and your bodies could not be recovered."

"But—" Shi Hua shook her head. "My aunt helped train me. She won't accept that excuse. She won't rest until—"

"No, she won't," Po said. The two men smiled at each other.

Of course. Shi Hua wanted to smack herself for her stupidity. Aunt Yin Li was already warming the bed of the emperor. "I see."

"Good to know you're as bright as Biming promised." The emperor grinned.

She scowled at him. "With all due respect, sir, I'm also bright enough to know I cannot always protect your brother alone. It took the assistance of three of my friends to save your brother and apprehend his attackers today. If I suddenly die shortly after saving Po, your enemies will know I'm the new person in his entourage. All this secrecy will be for naught."

The emperor leaned back and regarded her. "What are you suggesting?"

She shrugged. "It's no secret I humiliated the Reverend Father of Conflict at the Spring Rituals tournament. My own reverend father found it necessary to transfer me out of Jing to soothe Chen's ruffled feathers. Make the destination wherever you deem fit, but allow me to keep contact with my family so no suspicions are aroused."

Prince Po chuckled. "It's the best plan I've heard so far."

"Agreed." The emperor raised his cup to seal the arrangement.

Unfortunately, the appropriate mourning period meant the coronation, and therefore the prince's journey, were delayed until well into the late summer typhoon season. The rough seas made Shi Hua wish that Reverend Father Chen had lashed her after all. Though he had to be irked she had taken her vows early.

"First time on a ship, Sister Shi Hua?" the prince asked as she lay in their cabin.

"Yes, Your Highness—" Just that little effort sent her stomach into convulsions. She bent over the bucket again, but she had nothing left in her stomach.

"Luckily, our first stop is the Fire Islands in three days. In the spring, we will sail to the city of Orrin in Issura."

She frowned. The capital of the queendom was Standora. It would be more appropriate for someone of Prince Po's stature to be stationed closer to the seat of power. "Why there?"

"Many reasons, trade being foremost. But what else can you think of?"

"People will be freer with their tongues than they would at the capital."

The prince tapped his nose.

She stared at the wooden ceiling beams of the ship. "The School of Sorcery will insist on sending one of their members to guard you, Your Highness."

"Eventually, but we will worry when that happens. And you need to remember to address me as 'Your Excellency'. I'm officially an ambassador now." He kissed her forehead, no doubt practicing for her role as his concubine. "Get some rest if you can." He rose and stalked out of the cabin.

She closed her eyes and concentrated. *Mei Wen, are you busy?*

No. You sound like you're still across the street. How are you doing?

Other than typhoon season not agreeing with my stomach, fine.

Mei Wen's laughter tickled. *Thank you for convincing our temple heads to allow us to be involved. It has definitely soothed Jian and Fa's hurt feelings.*

If you don't mind, I need to cut this short. I'll talk with you in four days.

Good eventide, my friend.

Shi Hua pulled the blankets tighter. Adjusting from being Sister Shi Hua of the Temple of Light to Shi Hua, concubine of Ambassador Quan Po of Jing would be a challenge.

And despite her roiling stomach, she was looking forward to tackling that challenge.

Justice

The tinkling bells that lined her cloak announced the girl's presence as I ate my breakfast. "Justice Anthea, may I speak with you privately?"

Most Orrin inns were incredibly noisy, but the crowd here grew even more boisterous. It wasn't often a priestess of Love addressed a priestess of Balance in a public business. Not that I could tell if her cloak was the appropriate red silk. At least, not the way most people saw the color. But the clientele went out of their way to speak loudly and ignore us.

The dry musk of pigs underlaid her expensive perfume. I spooned the last bit of eggs into my mouth. Even if her odor hadn't given her away, she didn't bother to sit or give her name as an equal should.

Maybe she was too cocky about her deception. Or she was too frightened.

After dabbing the corners of my mouth, I smiled. I couldn't see her face with the heavy veil she wore, but I delayed long enough to detect her bare hands shift from dark gold to bright orange as they heated with her nervousness.

I should have waited for Luc to return from the bathhouse, but curiosity got the better of me. "Of course, sister." I held out my own hand, which she took and assisted me in rising from the bench. Just as anyone with decency, or the appearance of such, would help a blind woman to her lodging.

We carefully climbed the steps to the room Luc and I rented for the week, her to demonstrate her solicitude to the crowd in the common area, me to maintain the illusion of my sightlessness. Once we gained the second floor and I released my hold on the banister, my free hand slipped into the folds of my robes and grasped the handle of my dagger.

I led the way into the sleeping chamber.

"Justice, I have—"

To anyone else, my actions flowed so fast they would have seemed magic. With a swift kick, I shut the door. Before it slammed, I shoved the girl against the cheap plaster that covered the walls, my left forearm pressed against her throat. The tip of my dagger flipped up her veil before the point settled at the fragile join of her ear and jaw.

I didn't need her sharp gasp to know my hood had fallen back with the speed of my movements.

"Goddess, what are you?" The tremor in her voice matched the rapid throb of her artery under my blade. Everyone expected the milky white orbs of the sightless, like the rest of my order. Only Luc ever had the courage to tell me that no human's eyes were the color of blood.

"A better question is why a pig herder thought she could pass for a priestess of Love."

"Please forgive me, Justice. I didn't know how else to seek your help without the entire city—" Her sob could have been faked.

"You know the penalty for impersonating a priest or priestess of the Twelve," I ground out. "Who did you steal the robes from?"

"I didn't take them! They were my mother's."

I jerked away from the girl. I knew better than to release a potential threat. Thirty years of blasted training.

But her mother hadn't sold her. The way my mother had sold me at the tender age of three winters.

The hiss of steel on leather whispered on the other side of the door. No doubt the inn's patrons had enjoyed telling the story to Luc when he returned from his errand. I touched his mind and warned him of our guest. He sheathed his sword and slipped inside our room.

"Maybe you'd better start at the beginning, child." The rumble of his voice at my back reassured me.

The girl edged around me. "M'lord. I-I need your help. My betrothed has been kidnapped."

Wonderful. A cock-and-bull story. "Why haven't you gone to the magistrate's office?"

Her hair rustled as she looked at me, then back at Luc. "His own parents did the deed, Lord, Lady. He is Marco DiMara."

A bitter laugh erupted from my throat. A pig herder promised to the scion of one of the richest families in all of the land of Issura? "You really expect us to believe that load of—"

Luc cut me off. "You understand I will truth-bind you?"

"Yes, m'lord." It was the first time I heard confidence in the girl's voice.

In less than three heartbeats, Luc had muttered the words of his spell. Brilliant oranges, reds and yellows of active magic surrounded the girl. She sat on the edge of our bed. The slide of skin over skin as she rubbed her hands set my nerves on edge.

"I am Katarina DiLove. My mother kept me after my birth eighteen winters ago, and I served as her handmaid until her death from the wasting sickness last summer. I have no great magics, nor did I wish to stay at the temple.

"My small talent is in the care of animals. I am—" Her voice faltered as the spell prodded her. "Was apprenticed with Jovis, the city's veterinarian. I met Marco last fall. His horse had broken a leg in a hunting accident, and I healed the poor creature."

Luc whistled, a high, surprised sound. My estimation of the girl tilted. A true healer had more than a *little* talent.

Katarina didn't seem to notice our reactions. "He courted me. I told him I had no dowry than the death gift from my mother, but he said it didn't matter. That he loved me no matter the difference between our stations.

"I was to meet him at the Wilding God's clearing two nights ago. He wasn't there, but Lady DiMara was. She said that I would pay for seducing her son. That she and her husband would ensure I never saw him again. That if by happenstance we did meet, he would not know me.

"Yesterday morning, Master Jovis released me from my contract. He said I could sleep in the pig barn last night, but it would be best for both of us if I left the city."

Katarina's voice turned hard. "The DiMaras own the magistrate. He would not help if I had gone to him. High Brother Kam sent me to you."

"Disguised as a priestess?"

"No. That was my idea."

Once her story finished spilling. Katarina sucked in a wretched breath and began sobbing in earnest. I questioned her for nearly half of a candlemark, but her story did not alter one whit, nor could she give us more details.

I sat down next to the girl, her sobs now reduced to hiccups. She not so subtly scooted away. I couldn't fault her. The reaction to me, to my eyes, was due to my own foolishness.

"There may not be anything we can do," I said. "It may be as simple as Marco's parents threatening to disown him if he continues with his plans to marry you, and he buckled to their wishes."

"But Marco isn't like that!"

"We'll look into it. That is all I can promise." I reached into a pocket of my robes and produced two gold pieces. "Go to Nastine. That's the next stop on my circuit. Tell the adherents at the Temple of Balance there I sent you, and wait for me. Nothing more. I'll be there next week with my findings."

She bobbed her head. "It is more than I expected." After a moment's hesitation, she whispered, "About my own transgression, Justice—"

"I discover you've impersonated a priestess again, and I'll behead you myself."

"Yes, Justice." The acknowledgement was my only thanks. Luc received a hug from her before she fled through the sleeping room's door.

He sealed the door behind the girl and cast a privacy spell. Warmth filled me. I knew where his actions led.

"Well?" He unlaced the ties of my formal cloak.

I sighed as he eased the material from my shoulders. "The girl's only telling the truth as she knows it. She's low on facts and high on conjecture."

"A veterinarian is not going to release a true healer from her contract without cause. Or some damn good incentive." He pressed a tiny kiss along my neckline with each word, stroked the scars along my back.

"So you believe it bears investigation?"

He chuckled against my skin. "I know you. You would have her stripped and flogged for the impersonation if you suspected her story false. And since you've already pardoned one transgression this morning . . ."

I sighed as he unwound my breast band. "Whatever happened to the days when our vocations fought demons and otherworldly menaces instead of dealing with jilted lovers?"

"Maybe the Goddess is trying to teach you patience with boring cases."

I slapped at his hands. "Luc, we have to be at court by third morning." My protest was token, and we both knew it.

"It's only second hour. We have plenty of time." As if he cued them, the city bells rang.

I sighed and let him press me to the bedcovers.

The port city of Orrin was far too big not to have its own temple adjudicator. After the elderly resident justice had passed in the spring, the Reverend Mother assigned Orrin to my circuit. I couldn't say she ignored my entreaties or those of Kam, the old priest at the Temple of Light across the city's main thoroughfare. She always sent us both polite replies that she searched for the right candidate for the position.

Even though I spent a week out of every month in Orrin, I wasn't insane enough to take up residence in the temple facilities. The minute I did, the old hen would permanently assign me the position, and Luc and I would be parted forever. Besides, this city held too many bitter memories.

Per my usual, I heard the capital cases first that morning. I only had to execute one man. When I returned from the back courtyard after his beheading, I slipped my sword through the clasped hands of the Goddess's statue behind my chair. Odd how a bloody blade in the grip of a basalt figure subdued the crowd and kept order.

By the end of the afternoon, my grim humor had evaporated, and I wondered if I could die of boredom. The accused turned into a giant parade of disorderly conduct charges. At first evening, I called a halt to the proceedings.

The resident clerk approached me as the main hall cleared. "There's only a day and a half of civil cases left, m'lady." From her high voice and jovial attitude, she was still quite young.

I snorted. "And by morning, there will be another pile of criminal cases because some fleet arrived today, and all the crews decided to drink their pay."

She shrugged. "Sailors, m'lady."

Luc approached and handed me my cleaned sword. "Ready for evening meal?"

Bless him. The blade slid into my back scabbard with a satisfying *snick*. I had changed my clothes at the mid-day break, not that bloodstains were obvious in my traditional robes. Or so everyone said.

Even cold and dried, the spots left a slight temperature variation from the cloth. To me, they stood as mute badges to my position.

"Good eventide." I nodded to the clerk before Luc wrapped my arm around his.

As we stepped outside, I welcomed the cool air after the stuffiness of court. The business district's administrative offices and most of the temples were quiet for the night. Only the Temple of Love, three cross streets down, was brightly lit. The raucous laughter of men and the lighter giggling of the priestesses spilled from its front courtyard.

I paused, taking in the glow of oil lamps and torches. Then there were the sounds. Noises all too similar to the ones I made when Luc lay with me.

"Sentimental, Justice?" he whispered in my ear.

"No. I'm thankful my mother sold me every time I pass one of those places." She really had done me a favor though it felt like a wretched abandonment to the child I had been. But considering I couldn't keep my own vow of chastity to Balance—

I tugged on his arm, and we started across the street. "Come. I'm hungry." I left the rest of my feelings unsaid. It was too dangerous to speak the words aloud on an open street.

❖

Dinner with High Brother Kam was always a pleasant affair, but tonight, his jocularity seemed forced. After telling a particularly obscene story concerning a former mayor, two milkmaids, and a cow, he exhaled and sipped his wine.

He toyed with the stem for a long moment before he said, "I wish you would reconsider accepting the temple seat here in Orrin, Anthea."

I felt Luc's attention on me and I nodded my agreement. He rose and circled the room.

Brother Kam said nothing as Luc warded the room against anyone overhearing this conversation.

"Does this have anything to do with the DiMara family?" I asked.

Brother Kam's face blazed red. He reached for the wine pitcher and refilled his goblet. "According to the city's gossipmongers, Duke and Lady DiMara have been petitioning a match with one of the Queen's granddaughters for their son Marco. Needless to say, their attempts have been politely, but firmly, rebuffed.

He took a deep swallow of wine before continuing. "Three days ago, Marco came to me for advice on a young apprentice he was enamored with. Even though I told him to forget about her, he was quite insistent he loved her." A self-deprecating chuckle echoed from Kam's chest. "I asked him why he didn't seek the guidance of the priestesses down the street. He told me he needed straight answers, not flowery speech."

"And?" I prompted.

Brother Kam looked at me squarely, one of the few who knew the truth about me and was unafraid to gaze upon my failed attempt at sight. "I told him if he was serious, he would collect any money he could lay his hands on and flee with his paramour to Cant. Lady DiMara would never countenance a match between any of her children and a mere animal healer, much less a bastard child of the Spring Rituals."

He took another swallow of wine. "Yesterday, the veterinarian Jovis came to me. It was before noon, and the man was more intoxicated than adherents of the Mother at a harvest. The man *never* drinks because he never knows when he might be summoned." He slammed his hand against the surface of the table.

"What did he tell you?" Luc said.

"Nothing." Kam waved his hand in the air. "He couldn't tell me a bless-ed thing. He was under some kind of compulsion I could not break." He stared at the tapestry of Light decorating the far wall. "He tried. God help him, he tried to tell me, but I found a secondary spell designed to kill him if he managed to defeat the primary compulsion.

"This morning, Marco's paramour showed up on my doorstep."

Luc relayed our own encounter with Katarina. Kam grunted and poured another goblet of wine.

My palms formed a blade, and I rested my chin against my fingertips. "This doesn't make sense. Why go to such lengths to stop Marco?"

"Oh, the story gets better." Anger coated Kam's words. "Shortly after I sent Katarina to speak to you, Duke DiMara arrived, claiming Marco wishes to take temple vows."

"He's of age, is he not?" Luc said.

"Yes." Kam shook his head. "I cannot refuse an honest supplicant. But . . ."

Luc's own rage flicked at the back of my mind. Katarina's story fell into place. The DiMaras had set a very neat trap for their son.

None of the temples would condone a memory block of this type, not even those of the God of Thieves. Only a second-rate sorcerer would agree to such a perversity, therefore the spell would eventually fail. By the time poor Marco realized what had happened to him, he would be sworn to the God.

And only the Temples of Light and Balance required their priests and priestesses to remain chaste.

Coldness swept through me, though I wasn't sure if it was concern for the young lovers or mine and Luc's own violation of our vows. "Do you have the list of non-temple affiliated talents for Orrin?"

Kam pulled a scroll from his robes and handed it to Luc, who read off the names. Part of me was pleased Katarina had done the smart thing and registered. The rest of the practitioners listed bore some thought. They ranged from a minor prince with limited talent and no hope for the throne to several bastards from the other temples.

I stood. "Thank you for your hospitality, Brother Kam, but it is getting late."

"Thank you for listening to my nonsense." Relief danced along the old man's words. "If I can be of assistance . . ."

I squeezed his hand. "You've been more than enough help."

"Brother Luc?"

We paused at Kam's querulous tone. "Yes?"

"I'm grateful for your assistance, but my old bones cannot perform this office much longer. If Justice Anthea decides to settle in Orrin, may I present your name to the Reverend Father as my replacement?"

Luc tilted his head. "I would be honored, Brother."

Luc paced our room at the inn. Every curse word in the records poured from his mouth.

I sat cross-legged on the bed and rubbed my temples at the growing headache. His tirade was difficult to shut out, made meditation impossible. "Any hope that your tantrum will end soon?"

He paused in mid-step. "It's one thing when your parents sell you to the temples, but this—"

"Is illegal. I'm not disagreeing with you, but we need to find Marco before the memory block is performed. The DiMaras have had to rush, haven't thought out their plan thoroughly. And why punish Marco, instead of quietly killing Katarina? This type of revenge is too personal."

"A way to keep the other DiMara children in line? Make them work harder at seducing a member of the royal family?"

"Maybe. Read the names to me again."

The parchment rustled, a counterpoint to Luc's baritone as he repeated each name on the list. He tossed the scroll on the bed. "It's too many. We don't have time to check out each one. We can try a tracking spell on Marco."

I pressed my hands together and rested my elbows on my crossed knees. "If this unknown sorcerer has a lick of common sense and any real power, he is shielding both his presence and Marco's. If we try to track either of them, it will alert our unknown idiot that we're looking. And if he can't perform the memory block in time, he may decide slitting Marco's throat and fleeing is his best option for survival."

"The Wilding God's clearing? Lady DiMara?"

I smiled. "That was my thought."

The bells rang second night while we crossed the city. Black trousers and long-sleeved tunics allowed us to blend with the shadows. As for evading the night watch and accessing one of the city gates, three generations of peacetime in Issura made the men and women a little too complacent. Besides, they never expect anyone to *leave* the city this late.

Luc and I jogged to the clearing. While the Lord of Wild Things had an altar within every city, a copse outside of the walls was always set aside for him.

Luc stumbled twice on roots. For me, the blue trees and their yellow canopies were as bright as daytime. Sometimes I suspected he teased me when he claimed the trunks were brown and the leaves green to him. However, I had no doubt nighttime for him was like the dark to which I was born.

"Here?" he asked when we reached the clearing.

I looked up at the bright red owl perched on the branch above us. "Only if you want droppings down your collar."

Luc grunted and followed while I found an appropriate spot. I sat cross-legged, my hands on the grass beside my thighs and concentrated.

The matrons of my order say that in the beginning, the universe was perfectly balanced, and that in the end, perfect balance will be achieved again. Translated, their teachings meant we could see the past, and sometimes, even the future.

What we needed was two nights ago. Katarina's meeting with Lady Di-Mara.

Cold filled the glade as I plucked the strings of time. Luminous eyes and hot bodies surrounded us. This was not my Goddess's place, and the wild creatures watched.

Luc circled the glade, asking for the Wilding God's indulgence, while I rewound the last two sunsets. Ghostly figures, both human and animal, entered and left the holy circle. All of them walking, hopping, crawling backwards. I would have laughed if a young man's life and soul weren't at stake.

"There," Luc said. "Hold there."

I saw nothing but shadows. However, he moved quickly, marking the spot with his own magic.

"I have her trail."

At his affirmation, I let the threads of the past slip, and the world snapped back to the correct moment. We thanked Lord Wilding for his indulgence, and his children skittered and leapt back through the yellow foliage from whence they came.

The soft orange glow of Luc's spell disappeared down a different path than the one directly from the city. We followed it a short distance before it hit the National Road, the main route through the land. The same road we had arrived on only yesterday.

The tracking spell threaded north towards the capital and south toward the rest of the port cities along the coast. Luc cursed and kicked a cobblestone. I knew his words before he said them. "We shouldn't split up."

I set my fists on my hips. "Do you seriously believe each of us alone cannot handle our culprit, much less a petty, pampered aristocrat?"

He made a low sound of displeasure deep in his chest. "A candlemark. No more. We meet back here in two."

"Fine," I agreed before I pivoted and ran south.

⎯⎯◆⎯⎯

Near the end of the agreed candlemark, I despaired of finding the point of Lady DiMara's journey. Marco had to be relatively close in order to present him to Kam on the morrow.

I jogged around a bend in the road when the orange trail made a sharp right turn. The driveway would be nearly hidden by the foliage from most humans' sight as well as my own if not for Luc's spell.

I picked my way through the brush to the side of the drive but kept an eye on the trail. Through a break in the trees, a dark purple monolith rose from the bluffs. A manor house from its outline, yet I encountered no guards.

The gardens and yard were unkempt and overgrown. Since the DiMaras prided themselves on appearances, this could not possibly one of their holdings. Or had I totally misread the situation?

Above me, leaves rustled. I glanced up, half-expecting a night predator. Instead of the warm glow of a living creature, something cold black perched on the limb.

Something I'd never seen before.

I stepped away from the tree. More of these creatures gathered in the surrounding branches. Automatically, my hand reached for my sword hilt. The rasp of pulling the reinforced steel normally reassured me, but there was something *wrong* with these things.

Crickets stopped chirping. The rustling mice paused as they scavenged for seeds. The night itself seemed to hold its breath.

I swung as the first creature leapt. My sword connected, but the blow felt like nothing I experienced before. As if I'd struck stone, only to have the creature melt after jarring my arm.

Its fellows followed, and I found myself buried under a multitude of frigid bodies. When a fist struck my temple, it remained stone. I couldn't stop my fall into a different kind of blackness.

◆

Strange muttering infiltrated my aching head. I tried to raise my hand, only to find it fettered by cuffs linked to heavy chains.

"Oh, good. You're awake." The clap of pleasure sounded as loud as a crack of thunder directly overhead.

Very carefully, I pushed myself upright. Nausea threatened, but I couldn't afford to give in to my head injury. Taking stock, I found I had been left only with my trousers, tunic and undergarments. Matching shackles encircled my bare ankles.

Soft lavender light emanated from the walls, the same kind I'd seen on damp stones in caves. A man crouched before me, but my attention was drawn by one of the cold shadow creatures perched on a bookcase. Suspicion of what it may be gnawed on my gut.

The man unshielded a candle. The flare of white-hot light drove a spike of agony through my head, and I ducked my eyes against my shoulder.

"You react to light the same as a normal person. What are you, my dear?"

The tug to answer his question frightened me more than his shadow pets. He was definitely not as much as a fool as I'd thought if he'd laid a truthspell on me while I was unconscious.

"A human." To my relief, my answer did not result in a cascade of pain. He had the talent and knowledge to cast such a spell, but he hadn't been trained in logic or questioning.

His chuckle sounded like one of an elderly uncle indulging his favorite niece. "I mean, how did you get your unusual red eyes?"

"I gave them to myself."

"Why?"

I couldn't wiggle out of this answer. A bitter laugh poured from my lips. "It was my poor attempt over fifteen winters ago to restore my sight so I would be released from the Temple of Balance. I received ten lashes for the temerity to circumvent the Goddess's will."

His face turned from pale orange to crimson. All joviality fled him. "Who are you? What is your name? Your rank?"

Again, the pull on my soul to spill my secrets. If I resisted, he'd know I was hiding something, assuming the spell didn't kill me. Maybe, he'd think twice about his actions with the truth.

My chin lifted. "Justice Anthea, the circuit judge assigned to Orrin until the Reverend Mother of Balance names a permanent justice."

The man jumped to his feet. He must be younger than my original estimation.

From the bookcase, an odd, guttural noise came from the creature.

"No, you can't eat her," the man snapped. "Be silent. I need to think."

"Is that a demon?" I wanted my captor to say it wasn't. *Goddess, I take back this morning's jest with all my heat and soul.*

He ignored both of us, set the candleholder on a table, and started to pace the workroom.

Or dungeon, I decided. It was a good six strides long and an equal number in width. Deep blue chains hung at regular intervals along the wall to which I was shackled.

I tried to call for Luc, but my mental shout bounced off the shielding spell. It only added to the ache in my head. The demon, for surely that is what it was, growled. Since he'd already decided he wanted to eat me, I took his warning under due consideration.

Interesting that I didn't recognize it, but the descriptions of demons were based on normal human sight. I needed to add my observations about complete lack of body heat to the temple's chronicles. If I survived the night, that was.

From the occasional word I picked out from my captor's muttering, he had schemed as far ahead as Duke and Lady DiMara. Which is to say, barely at all.

"Might I make a suggestion?"

He halted and from the odd feeling on the back of my neck, he glared at me. "What?"

"You were planning to block Marco DiMara's memory. If you haven't yet, you should cast the spell on us both."

"Why would I do that?"

I was correct in my original assessment that he was an idiot. However, it didn't make him any less dangerous, and I needed to buy time for Luc to find us.

I sighed. "If neither Marco nor I remember you, you cannot be charged with kidnapping or holding us prisoner. We both live, and you'll still get your payment from Lady DiMara."

"I already received my payment in advance. I am not stupid."

I sent a silent prayer of thanks to the Goddess that he didn't phrase his words in the form of a question. "And you won't be hunted like a dog for murdering a priestess," I pointed out.

He turned to the demon. "Bring the youth in here, and do *not* eat him."

The demon jumped down from the bookcase. Instead of exiting the room properly, it seemed to dissolve before it slid through the crack between the door and the frame. Interesting. Hopefully, the creature would take the time to open the door when it returned with Marco, or my efforts to keep the boy alive would be for nothing.

"What is your name, sir?"

"Uhn-uh." My mysterious sorcerer waggled his index finger. "I'm not falling for that."

I gave him a smile, as polite of one as I could muster. "I would need your true name to cause any mischief." I shrugged. And became painfully aware of a huge bruise on my shoulder. However, I didn't let the smile waver. "Besides, I won't remember the name you give me anyway."

"Who knows you are here?"

My smile fell. "Only you and your demons," I said. Thank the Goddess, he couldn't properly ask a question. "All you have to do is leave me on the National Road with the gear I came with, and you'll be perfectly safe."

He made a derisive sound. "If you are a circuit justice, where is your partner priest of Light?"

I clenched my jaw. The pain started in my belly, similar to eating the obscenely hot peppers of the arid regions of Cant. It quickly escalated to what I suspected a glowing poker shoved through my gut would feel like. I fell to my side. My body curled into a ball. "Heading north on the road, tracking Lady DiMara," I gasped.

"Stupid, stupid bitch."

It took a moment for his meaning to penetrate the dissipating haze of pain while he shouted for his demons. He referred to the noblewoman, not me.

I pushed myself back to a sitting position. If only he'd leave the dungeon, I could pull out one of my remaining hairpins and pick the Goddess forsaken locks.

Instead, the door swung open with such force, it crashed into the stone wall. Two of the demons dragged in a struggling man. I was sure the third demon behind them was the one who desired to pick his teeth with my bones.

From the hot bruises on the man's face and hands, he'd fought his captors. He shouted imprecations at the demons with every step they took until he was chained next to me.

"Marco, it will be all right."

He grew silent at my attempted reassurance and addressed our captor. "Are you insane, Samael? Did my mother pay you to kidnap her as well?"

Now, I had a name. One Luc had read from the list.

"Shut your mouth," Samael shrieked. "Or I'll have the demons eat your tongue."

I stared at him. "Samael DiRoy. Youngest son of the Crown Prince. Scholar and herbalist. Magical talent limited to languages." *Goddess help us, he had the demons place the spells on the veterinarian Jovis.* "How in the names of the Twelve did you manage to summon demons?"

"Jealous because I can, Priestess?" he hissed.

"Not particularly." I winced as I replied. *Bloody Sword, this truthspell will be the death of me.* "Actually, I'm impressed. All such texts were supposedly destroyed by the Temples a century ago."

My fawning tone hit his ego just right. "I found a tome tucked away in the rare books section of the capital library. I translated a few phrases, realized it was a grimoire on the forbidden magics, and I smuggled it out."

"But, Prince Samael, why bother with this child—" I gestured at Marco "—when you can *command demons?*"

"I need the money." His boasting shifted into whining. "Do you have any idea of how expensive summoning and feeding these things are?"

An awful suspicion grew in me. "Do Marco's parents know about the demons?"

"Of course." Samael's confidence chilled me more thoroughly than the demons' touch.

"Holy Mother," Marco swore. "They want you to raise a demon army for them once I'm out of the way."

I wanted to kick the youth for giving voice to my fears. We were both dead now.

Samael slowly shook his head. "I'm so sorry. For both of you. I'll make this as easy as possible." He pulled a knife from the worktable.

My dagger.

I curled and pretended to cower against the wall. I prayed there was enough slack in my chains, prayed that the stories I heard as a child of the demons' weaknesses were true. I had to be faster than the three demons in the room.

He approached me and reached for my hair. I slammed my heels into his knees. With a sickening crunch, tendons tore and bones shattered. He screamed. My dagger slipped from his hand as he collapsed and clattered against the stone floor.

I swept one of the arm chains around his throat and yanked him against my chest. The first demon, the one who wanted to taste my flesh crouched inches from our faces.

"Back away, or I snap his neck," I growled.

It huffed before it said something to the others in their guttural language. All three edged away from us. Their actions confirmed one of the old tales. They needed the sorcerer who summoned them alive in order to remain in this plane.

And if I killed a member of the royal family without benefit of a trial, I'd find my neck on the business end of another justice's sword.

The problem of getting Marco and myself out of this dungeon persisted. I rolled the possibilities through my mind, a process that became more difficult by the moment for reasons that had nothing to do with Samael's hoarse cries. With a sickening realization, I understood my situation. My head injury was worse than I originally suspected. Blood pooled inside my skull, and the growing pressure would kill me if we didn't escape soon.

"Where's the key?" I tightened and released the chain to gain his attention.

"If I tell you, you'll kill me," he whimpered.

Telling the idiot he was dead already wouldn't improve the situation. "I can grant you clemency if you cooperate," I said through clenched teeth.

"Don't bargain with him, Justice."

From the corner of my eye, I found Marco had already picked the locks to his wrist cuffs. Goddess bless the boy. He'd had the presence of mind to snatch my dagger when it fell.

The steel would be ruined once he was finished, but I didn't care. It was by far the least of our worries.

Marco quickly released the locks on my shackles while I kept a tight hold of the chain around Samael's neck. He stayed close to me when the demons started muttering under their breath.

"I need your help to lift him," I whispered.

Marco was no dandy. He hauled the sorcerer upright, and Samael screamed at the pressure on his ruined knees.

I gained my feet, only a rush of vertigo threatened to knock me down again. Clutching the wall, I made my way to the worktable. Relief swept through me when my fingers wrapped around the pommel of my sword. Feeling around the wooden surface produced a great many objects, none of which were my boots or the sword's sheath. We couldn't waste any more time.

"Stick to the wall," I muttered.

"Yes, m'lady." Marco replaced the chain with his arm and dragged the sorcerer, keeping him between us and the demons.

"Over there." I pointed at the opposing corner with my sword. The stones were only cold under my right foot. My left was numb.

The first demon spat an obvious insult, but he and his fellows edged around the dungeon while we made our way to the door. The instant we were through, I slammed the door shut and slid the iron bolt into place. The heavy wood shivered as the demons threw themselves against it. The barrier wouldn't last long. Once the demons let go of their rage, they'd remember they could slip through the cracks.

Somehow, we climbed the stairs and exited the front door of the manor house. We backed slowly down the drive, the young nobleman literally dragging the screaming sorcerer. My own footing became more unsure.

"They're coming," Marco murmured.

Black shadows climbed the surrounding trees and swung through branches toward us.

I'd never killed someone without an appropriate trial. A growing disquiet said Samael's death would be the only way for Marco to survive. Deep down, I acknowledged I would never be greeted by the goddess at my passing, much less make it back to Orrin

"Luc, I'm so sorry," I whispered.

Anthea!

Luc. I nearly collapsed when the pounding of hoofs raced toward us from the main road.

"Marco!"

I recognized the feminine voice that shouted. The name was out of my reach. I'd sent her away, hadn't I?

"Here!" For all our shouting, the cold shadows would reach us before Luc. I couldn't fight them off before. I couldn't let an innocent die.

"Drop him, Marco."

The boy complied, and the sorcerer shrieked.

"Samael DiRoy, you have been charged with using forbidden magic by your own admission." My hands shook. I wished it were rage and fear instead of my injury.

"I, Marco DiMara, hereby affirm the justice's account, having heard the confession myself." The ritual response of a priest of Light.

I wanted to weep with relief. Marco was a good boy. A smart boy. I hoped he'd find his happiness.

Luc. So many things I wanted to say to him. So many things he needed to know.

A wave of frigid air hit me. "Samael DiRoy, you are found guilty of using forbidden magic. The sentence is death."

Wordless cries were his only answer. Marco held him down by the shoulders.

I prayed the old stories were true. That the demons hadn't tricked me in the dungeon.

I slammed my sword point into the base of Samael's skull. Shrieks of demon outrage echoed through the woods. With muffled pops, the black shadows disappeared from this plane of existence.

Hands caught me as I pitched forward over the corpse of my deadly idiot. My last thought was that I was finally *free.*

The scent of vanilla and cinnamon twined around me. My eyes fluttered open. The dark blues and greens of a marble ceiling met my gaze.

"Where am I?" My voice was a hoarse croak.

"You're in the bedroom of the Justice of Orrin. Here, drink this." Familiar hands held up my head.

I gratefully sipped the water.

"Do you have a headache?"

I had to think about it since my entire head seemed to be wrapped in cotton. "No." Recognition slipped into place.

Luc.

"Good. Katarina needed to eat and sleep. The girl hasn't left your side. She's beside herself with guilt for putting you at the mercy of demons."

"She—" It took me a moment to pull the threads of memory from the tangled skein my mind had become. "I sent her to Nastine."

"She disobeyed you and went to Kam again."

Luc filled in the events after I'd executed Samael and passed out. He returned to the city after he searched for me and spotted a demon watching the road. He gathered as many wardens from the temples as he could. Katarina insisted on accompanying the rescue party.

Which turned out to be fortunate, or unfortunate from my point of view, since she kept me alive long enough for them to return me to Orrin and find a trained healer.

The senior physician of Orrin insisted she become his apprentice since Master Jovis had released her. Samael's death dissolved the demons' compulsion on Jovis, who denied he'd terminated her contract willingly. Just another civil matter on the docket.

Luc's companions hadn't found the grimoire Samael used at the abandoned manor house. The Temples of Thief and Wilding worked together and tracked the blasted thing to Duke and Lady DiMara's estate. They had been captured after a brief fight between their household retainers and the temple wardens.

"And me?" I whispered.

"Technically, you're under house arrest for the murder of a member of the royal family. The Reverend Mother of Balance arrives later tonight. The trials will be tomorrow."

The noise from the crowds that thronged outside of the Temple of Balance echoed in the cavernous interior until the Reverend Mother ordered the main doors closed. A trial for treason outside of the capital was unusual. Two on the same day was unprecedented. In such severe matters, the highest-ranking priest or priestess of each of the Twelve Temples of Orrin sat as one.

Like the DiMaras, I stood in the accused box, stripped of all accoutrements of my rank. Instead, I wore a plain gray shift. No hood covered my face this time. The whispers were equally divided by the DiMaras attempt to seize the throne through dark magic and my appearance. Even the wardens guarding us looked uneasy.

I could feel Luc sitting with the rest of the spectators, but I didn't dare look in his direction. The milky white eyes of the Reverend Mother bore into me for a moment before she banged the hilt of her sword on the altar to begin the proceedings.

The first trial took less than a candlemark

Brother Kam stood and read the verdicts. The only thing that saved Duke DiMara from a death sentence was he didn't know about the demons, and he certainly didn't know his wife had stolen the grimoire from Samael. The demons had convinced her she was a much better overlord than the sorcerer.

Duke DiMara hung his head and wept quietly as the wardens escorted him from the court. Lady DiMara screamed obscenities until the Reverend Mother ordered her taken to the back of the temple.

"As the persons immediately wronged by the actions of the guilty, I hereby order that all titles, possessions and estates of the guilty, minus the tithe to the crown, pass to Marco and Katarina DiMara." She leaned back in her chair. "I suppose congratulations are in order."

I closed my eyes and sent a prayer of thanks to the Twelve for watching over the two lovers.

"Anthea DiLove, you have been charged with treason by way of murder, specifically Lord Samael DiRoy, third cousin to our beloved liege." She used my birth origin name, a reminder that I had no title when accused of crimes against the crown.

I opened my eyes and raised my chin. I'd done what I had to save Marco from being forced into temple life as Luc and I had been. Or worse, eaten by the demons. I wouldn't—I couldn't—change a thing.

"Lady Justice, may I speak on behalf of the accused?" There was a twinge of nervousness in Marco's voice.

"Both Brother Luc and Anthea DiLove have given their statements in this matter, Duke DiMara." Unlike the boy's, the Reverend Mother's tone was ice cold and steady.

"As have I, m'lady." He crossed from the witness area to stand in front of the judges. "If it weren't for Justice Anthea's quick thinking, we'd be neck deep in another demon war. Surely this court can take the good of her actions into account. Justice should be tempered by mercy."

"Do you presume to lecture me in my own hall?"

Everyone, including the rest of the judge's panel cringed at the echoes against the marble.

"No, m'lady. I ask for clemency. Orrin has been without a permanent justice for a quarter of a year. I swear responsibility if you would appoint Justice Anthea."

"No!" I shouted. Nausea threatened. Surely the demons had hit Marco on the head as well.

The gallery of spectators erupted at my outburst. The Reverend Mother pounded her sword pommel repeatedly for order before the crowd settled.

"Do you understand what you are offering, child?"

"Should she commit any further offenses, I will share in her punishment." This time, his voice rang out like a confident nobleman's.

The Reverend Mother turned to me. "Anthea DiLove, you have tried to escape service to our goddess from the time you could use a privy by yourself. You should know by now it is not that easy." Gleeful satisfaction danced in her words. "Unless any of my colleagues have objections?"

A collective murmur of agreement issued from her fellow judges.

"Anthea DiLove, you are hereby sentenced to serve as the chief justice of the Temple of Balance for the city of Orrin for the remainder of your natural life."

Four days later, Luc and I were riding to Nastine. The Reverend Mother gave me a week to catch up on the town's caseload before I was required to return to Orrin. He and I took a little used track instead of the National Road. We had too much to discuss.

"What if we took all the money we can lay our hands on and head south to Cant?" I tilted my head upward, enjoying the caress of the summer sun.

Luc laughed, a hearty sound that flushed birds from the surrounding foliage. "You can't do that anymore than I could."

"Someone will find out about us eventually," I pointed out. "If you take the permanent position in Orrin, discovery is even more likely."

"What makes you think someone doesn't already know?" His words were so soft I barely heard them over the clomping of the horses' hooves.

"I don't understand."

"Why didn't you have Katarina flogged for impersonating a priestess?"

His change of subject threw me off. "That had nothing to do—"

"Maybe it does. So why didn't you?"

It wasn't a truthspell that tugged at my heart. "Maybe because I hoped someone would show us compassion someday." Then I understood.

Neither of us said anything more the rest of the ride to Nastine.

Diplomacy in the Dark

I didn't bother to hide my displeasure at my early morning guests. Even my staff here in the Temple of Balance had learned not to disturb me in the mornings before my second cup of tea in the four months since I'd been permanently assigned here.

Well, sentenced depending upon one's point of view.

However, I did alter my footsteps so I didn't stomp into the receiving room as a disgruntled child would. It was inappropriate for the chief justice of Orrin.

Despite decorum, I didn't wait for my head warden, Little Bear, to announce me. I shoved open the doors, and the two men inside jumped to their feet.

"Magistrate DiCook, I truly hope His Grace is not telling you that interrupting my breakfast is acceptable behavior."

The magistrate stiffened. Whether it was from my appearance or my tone, I couldn't tell. I rarely bothered wearing my hood indoors since everyone in the city of Orrin learned of my unusual appearance and that I was sighted during my trial at the beginning of summer.

Knowing my eyes discomfited the magistrate, my action was a petty maneuver on my part. But he had tried to run roughshod over me since my appointment to the temple seat. Of course, his behavior might have something to do with my investigation of him in connection to the previous duke's high treason.

"Arturo, the captain of the *Mar Tranquilus* has been murdered, Justice Anthea." If Duke Marco DiMara's anger wasn't evident in his voice, the surge of orange through his normal golden appearance marked the emotion. It also explained the crimson cast of the magistrate.

The duke's family controlled a majority of Orrin's merchant fleet since the end of the last demon invasion over a century ago. Of course, he'd take the death of the master of his flagship personally.

I clasped my hands behind my back. "I am certain the magistrate and his peacekeepers will present me with all evidence along with the culprit when they capture him, Your Grace."

"Therein lies the problem, Justice." DiCook actually sounded uncomfortable. "I'm not sure the captain was murdered."

"You can't tell me that a man freezes to death in his heated cabin before winter by accident," Marco snapped.

I immediately regretted not having my second cup of morning tea, and I suppressed the urge to rub my forehead from the headache I no doubt would have before the matter was complete. "From the beginning, please, my lords."

"The *Mars Tranquilus* was scheduled to dock shortly before dawn," Marco started. His four short months as the Duke of Orrin as well as his recent marriage had given the youth a measure of maturity. "They were returning from a run from Jing."

A frown tugged the corners of my mouth. "Now?"

Marco shrugged. "The weather oracle predicted one more major storm in two weeks. Arturo believed it was sufficient time."

Only the bravest, the most experienced, or the most insane of merchant sailors tried to squeeze in a trip to the Far West between the autumn typhoons and the winter squalls.

"And?" I prompted. DiCook remained quiet which bothered me more than I cared to admit.

Marco forced out a harsh breath. "Prior to the trip, Arturo and I had discussed his first mate Titus's readiness for a command of his own. So, Arturo was in his quarters, and Titus brought the ship to dock. He discovered the captain's body when he went to make his report."

I measured my words before speaking. As much as I found the duke's company pleasant, he could react brashly. "Your Grace, if Captain Arturo died of exposure, that does not constitute murder."

"You misunderstand, Justice," DiCook finally spoke. "He was discovered on the floor of his cabin frozen as solid as any hank of meat in the middle of a Gray Mountains winter. The coals in the cabin brazier still glowed when

I boarded the ship for the initial query. There is also the matter of a small casket found next to the body that wasn't listed on the captain's manifest."

"And it wasn't listed on the contract either," Marco spat out. "Sorcery has to be involved considering the manner of Arturo's death, which makes it murder."

"Unless he was smuggling an illegal magical object," DiCook snapped back. "And accidentally killed himself with it."

I swallowed a sigh. Obviously, the two men had been at odds about the discrepancies long before they arrived at my temple. Normally, I could dump a minor contractual matter on the Temple of Light, but the investigation of an unusual death landed on me, regardless of the sorcery question. "And the casket was not a personal effect of the captain or one of the crew members?"

"No, and whatever was in it was missing." Triumph tinged the magistrate's voice.

"And how do you know there was something in the casket, Magistrate?"

He shifted, uncomfortable at my questioning his abilities again. "A small velvet bag lay next to the captain. It had the duke's crest on it."

I turned to Marco, who lifted his chin. "It's the same type my ships use to pack jewels, but there were none sent and none supposed to be on the return trip."

"So we have an unusual death and a possible theft of an unknown item," I said.

"And smuggling," the magistrate added.

Marco's color flared from orange to scarlet. "That's a lie."

DiCook's color shifted from deep crimson to bright scarlet as well. "I'm sure, given the DiMara penchant for honest dealings—"

"That's enough, Magistrate," I ordered, adding a little hint of magic to make my voice louder and deeper. "I will need to collect a priest from the Temple of Light—"

"Brother Luc is already at the docks," DiCook growled. "He along with a junior priest are questioning the crew."

Relief that Luc was already involved tugged at the knot my miniscule morning meal had become in my stomach. I had a feeling someone would die before the end of the day, and I didn't relish being the executioner.

The autumn air was crisp with a hint of ocean tang. I would have preferred walking to our destination, but Little Bear had insisted on riding to the dock where the *Mar Tranquilus* was berthed, as well as bringing a full escort of Balance wardens.

I was loath to admit the additional guards were a good idea. My attempt as a youth to give myself sight to escape temple life hadn't worked as I planned. Since I was born blind, I had no reference. My version of sight from my inept spell relied on the difference in the heat of objects. Shortly after dawn, the measure of warmth between the docks, the ships and the water were so close that I could have walked off the pier if it weren't for Little Bear by my side as we marched past the peacekeepers and up the wooden ramp to the top deck.

The ship's compliment milled on the quarterdeck, all golds and bright oranges, muttering under their breath. Resentment filtered through my mental shields. And grief. But the hardened sailors would never display that emotion openly. It twisted in their minds to anger.

When they caught sight of me and I deliberately pushed back my hood, their murmurs grew louder. Fear replaced their other emotions. The milky orbs of any other justice they could understand. According to Luc, my eyes were the color of blood to normal folks, and that was unnatural.

As unnatural as the death of their captain on board their ship.

I headed for the stern where the newest of the Temple of Light's priests stood between the rest of the crew and the spot where Luc interrogated a man, who must be Titus, the first mate, from the faint emblem on his vest. "Brother Jeremy."

"Lady Justice. We've questioned the rest of the crew. Brother Luc is finishing now." The young man's relaxed manner made it easy to like him.

The fact that his personal feelings had never seeped past his own shields made it easier to work with him.

I observed Luc with the first mate under his truthspell, their voices too soft to understand between the sea birds and the harbor activity increasing now that the sun was above the mountains. The resentment of the other sailors danced along the edge of my mental perception. The duke and the magistrate fidgeted on the edge of my physical perception.

Finally, the slight itch of active magic faded. With a furtive glance at me, Titus stood and stomped past us to join the rest of the crew.

I approached Luc, trailed by my unwanted guests. As much as I desired to sooth the fatigue I felt from him, I didn't dare touch him in front of an audience. "What are the results of questioning?"

"And a pleasant morn to you, too, Justice," he said dryly.

Brother Jeremy emitted a noise that sounded suspiciously like a stifled laugh.

I nodded. "Forgive my rudeness, Brother. I find my morning meal is repeatedly interrupted here."

"The citizens of Orrin do not have my years of experience. They'll learn not to come between you and your meals. And most especially your tea."

A snicker from Marco joined Jeremy's choked laughter.

"I'm so pleased the nobles and the priesthood find a man's death amusing," DiCook growled.

"We beg your pardon, Magistrate," Luc murmured. He always had a better rapport with people than I did. "To answer your question, Justice, none of the crew are involved with the captain's death. Only the first mate was aware of the casket. The captain brought it on board shortly before they set sail for home. He did not know the contents, and the captain refused to disclose such information when he asked."

"What about the casket's ultimate destination?"

"Titus only knows that Captain Arturo was to deliver it to an official at the Jing ambassador's palace."

"Has anyone touched the body?"

"Only the first mate and Magistrate DiCook." *Titus took a layer of skin off his fingers checking the captain's throat for breath or a heartbeat. DiCook was wise enough to use gloves. This matter frightens the water out of both the sailors and the peacekeepers,* Luc added silently.

Any talent among the crew?

The navigator has an infallible sense of direction, and the pilot can predict weather within three days. Both are registered. Luc didn't have to add there was no possible way their respective magical skills could freeze a man solid.

I steeled myself for what came next. "You can release your crew for leave, Your Grace."

"No!" DiCook stepped between the duke and me. "They were onboard when the captain was murdered."

"Now it's murder, Magistrate?" I tilted my head and smiled. "Unless you can tell me how the brothers of Light failed in their queries of the crew, it's better they disembark so they're not underfoot."

His breath came out in short, yellow blasts, but he said nothing.

Marco strode to the assembled men and dismissed them. Their grumbling subsided when the duke told them they would be paid for their lost day of work since the reason was not their fault.

Once the ship was clear, Luc led me to the captain's cabin. A purplish-black form lay on the wooden planks between the bunk and the desk. But it was the color of the open casket next to him that raised the fine hairs on the back of my neck. I'd only seen that hue of black once in my life, the night the duke and I met.

It was the color of demons.

I silently shared my suspicions with Luc. He cursed under his breath in Cantish, and my own tongue wanted to join him. I whirled around so fast, all of the men except Luc jumped. "Your Grace, you need to get your sailors back here now!"

Luckily, the duke caught his men before they reached the end of the dock. There was more grumbling and a few obscene gestures when I made the men strip down. And two threats when we searched their pockets and purses. Little Bear answered those with a polite offer to spend the night in a cell back at our temple.

Meanwhile, Luc and Jeremy combed every nook and cranny of the vessel with their magic. According to ancient tomes of our raised writing in the Balance library I'd read obsessively during my free time over the past four months, the Light priests' power was one of the few effective deterrents to a demon incursion. Luc verified the same in their library. But the men's power failed to flush out anything more than a dozen rats.

Two candlemarks later, we were back in the captain's cabin. This time, the first mate Titus joined us while Little Bear and my wardens kept an eye on the peeved, and re-clothed, sailors on the quarterdeck. Since all crew members were accounted for and none of them carried a demon, we were back at the beginning of the puzzle.

I suppressed a shiver at the reminder of a demon's frigid touch.

The possibility of demon magic killing the captain was a tempting conclusion, but I could miss other clues if I wasn't careful. And I had missed a major one by not checking the cabin before releasing the crew for leave.

I sat on the floor between the dead man and the cursed object, contemplating our next move. Arturo's body hadn't thawed one finger since sunrise, even though it had turned into an unseasonably warm autumn day. My attempt to rewind the past, to discover what had happened in his quarters, failed. Probably due to the proximity to the demon-infected casket, but I wouldn't allow anyone remove it.

"Has anyone touched the casket?" My words almost sounded normal. I had made a plentitude of mistakes in my life, but I may have just made my worst one yet by letting a demon loose in Orrin.

"I didn't touch anything, except the corpse," DiCook proclaimed.

"Nor I, my lady," Titus added.

"Who has been onboard and left since the ship docked?" I didn't need either priest to truthspell the other men. DiCook's face faded to a sickly yellow.

"Just the magistrate and me, m'lady." Marco's voice sounded as nauseated as I felt.

"We were together the whole trip to the Temple of Balance," DiCook said. "Surely one of us would have noticed something unusual about the other. And that's assuming any creature larger than a kitten could fit in that casket."

"They can change their shape and their appearance." Marco's voice was haunted from our encounter with the ones summoned by the queen's cousin. The ones that served his mother. The ones she would have allowed to eat his body and soul if we hadn't stopped them.

If I hadn't stopped them by illegally killing their summoner without a trial.

"Once it knew we were searching for it, maybe it attached itself to one of the peacekeepers or wardens," Jeremy offered.

Rolling the problem over and over in my head was making it ache even worse. "I would have seen it."

"Then the crew would have, too," DiCook snapped.

Luke tried to be reasonable. "No, they wouldn't have. The demons' abilities mean they can change their appearance to fool those of us with normal sight. Unless they can also change their essential nature, Justice Anthea would see them."

Titus cleared his throat. "Why are you all assuming the demon was on board since we left Jing? What if it were waiting for the ship's arrival?"

Everyone crammed in the cabin, including me, stared at the first mate.

His coloring brightened at our scrutiny, and he shrugged. "We brought the ship into port right at first light. Between the shadows and all of the crew busy dealing with the rigging, lines and anchor, a creature as black as both His Grace and Lady Justice described could have slipped onboard, killed the captain and escaped with gods' know what was in that casket."

"Brilliant. Simply brilliant." I smiled at Titus, which bothered him even more than my original attention. My knees complained of being in the same position for too long as I climbed to my feet. "It's time we spoke with the person for whom the casket was intended."

"You really intend to take that thing to the Jing ambassador's palace?" Luc cocked his head as he regarded me.

The idea I had was a slim chance to discover what led to Captain Arturo's death. "Do you or Brother Jeremy see anything unusual about the casket?"

Both priests shook their heads.

"Good." I turned to Marco. "Your Grace, can you procure—"

"Yes, most definitely." He darted out of the cabin.

Luc shook his head as I told them my plan. "You are mad."

"You will think I am more so." I faced Titus. "Would you like the opportunity to discover your captain's killer?" He opened his mouth, but I held up a hand to forestall his answer. "Before you agree, understand this. I will do everything in my power to protect you, but this visit to the Jing ambassador will be dangerous. Demons can make themselves as thin as air or as solid as an anvil. You will not be able to fight them as you would another human. If I tell you to run, then *you run*. Straight to the Temple of Light and find Brother Kam. He'll know what to do."

I thanked the Goddess that Luc's predecessor had remained at their temple in an advisory capacity. He knew everything we learned or had discovered concerning demons.

"Are you calling me a coward, Justice?" The low vibration of Titus' voice would have been a warning if I actually believed he'd raise a hand to me.

"I want you to enter this escapade of your free will and with full knowledge," I answered. "If there is a demon residing inside Ambassador Quan's residence, we may all die before the sun sets."

Titus gave a curt nod. "I understand, m'lady. However, if I may be so bold, we have no idea of what was in the original casket."

I smiled. "That's exactly how we will flush out our culprit."

The midday bells rang at the temples as we arrived at the Diplomatic Corridor. The mansions were more stately than those of the richest merchants, yet slightly less ostentatious than those of the minor nobles. Nearly every major power of the Far West and the Long Continents had a presence in Orrin since we were the second largest port city of Issura.

Titus rode beside me, dressed in the rich clothing of a prosperous merchant captain. We had to make do with a few things from Arturo's trunk, but the first mate was a bit wider in the shoulders and narrower in the hips. Both DiCook and Marco fretted about his appearance. Titus skewered them with the logical point that if he'd just been made master of his own ship, he wouldn't have had time to have new clothes tailored.

Curious stares from all the embassies followed us down the street. As the heads of our respective temples, Luc and I stuck out in the normal traffic of messengers and business people. Both the duke and the magistrate had wanted to send additional guards with us, but we insisted only one escort each. Anymore and we would be inviting a diplomatic incident.

Or too many questions.

As if we weren't courting both already with my insane plan.

We dismounted outside the entry of the Jing embassy, but before any of us could ring the bell, the iron-reinforced wooden gate swung open. A single guard in quilted leather and cloth armor bowed deeply, held upright only by his firm grip on his spear.

"The ambassador welcomes such distinguished company." He straightened. "May His Excellency offer the comfort of his stables for your steeds?"

I returned his bow. "Many thanks for your lord's graciousness. We are merely escorting the captain of the *Mars Tranquilus*. He has a most important package to deliver to Ambassador Quan."

Little Bear took the reins of the five horses. He had been given his orders to raise the alarm if we didn't return in half a candlemark. I had already dispatched the other three Balance wardens to warn the other temples that a demon-related item had been discovered aboard the ship.

The Jing guard bowed again. "This way, Lady Justice."

Titus grasped a replica of the casket firmly in both hands as we followed the guard into the courtyard. Luc and Jeremy trailed behind us.

I prayed to Balance no one else in the embassy could tell the difference between our artifice and a demon-tainted object. An extra prayer to the Goddess begged that the resident sorcerer could not detect the dormant spell I placed inside our replica.

Worry plucked my nerves. There were no guarantees my idea would work. I didn't have a demon to practice on.

From the corner of my vision, a faint line of green developed at Titus' hairline. I couldn't blame him for his anxiety. A thin trickle of sweat traced the skin down my own spine.

The rich aroma of the midday meal reached my nose before the guard led us into a great room. Rounds tables lined the side walls with a plentitude of people from various nations. At the far end, the ambassador sat at a rectangular table on a raised dais. The better to observe his guests I was sure.

The room grew quiet at our entrance except for the occasional curious whisper.

We reached the dais. A court sorcerer sat on the ambassador's right. A concubine on the left. It was the jewel at her throat that drew my attention. A deep black that swallowed the heat of the room. I silently shared my observation with Luc and Jeremy.

It appears to be a sapphire in our sight. The size of a hen's egg, Luc replied.

My suspicion of what had been in Captain Arturo's casket congealed. But why was the concubine wearing it?

Ambassador Quan didn't bother rising. The two priests and I didn't bother bowing. Titus followed our example.

"Lady Justice." Quan made a show of wiping his lips. His thin beard and moustache, a tradition of his homeland, shivered as he smiled. "I'm afraid I have no more seats available for you and your men to join our repast. If you would care to join me for a private dinner . . ."

I returned his smile. "I would never insult Your Excellency by subjecting his meager hospitality to my greater appetites."

ANTHEA!

I managed not to wince at Luc's mental reprimand, but I'd heard enough rumors about the ambassador's tastes from the Temple of Love to boil my blood.

Instead of taking offense, Quan chuckled. "Perhaps one day you might care to enlighten me. However, that is not the reason for your visit."

I inclined my head in Titus's direction. "An official from your great land gave the captain of the *Mars Tranquilus* a last minute item to be delivered directly to an official at your embassy. Unfortunately, the captain died in route, and he did not share the recipient with his crew."

Quan's attention focused on the former first mate. "If Captain Arturo passed, who might you be?"

His remark left an uneasy feeling in my gut. How many other Orrin ship masters was the ambassador keeping an eye on?

Titus subtly straightened. "The new captain of the *Mars Tranquilus* by His Grace, the Duke of Orrin's leave, Your Excellency."

Smart man. He didn't give his name in front of a strange sorcerer. Arturo trained him well.

"Forgive my lack of knowledge, m'lord," Titus continued. "As the Lady Justice said, the captain left no instructions as to this." He raised the casket slightly and lowered it. "I sought her advice on the matter and she offered to escort me to your residence."

Quan stroked the ends of moustache. "That doesn't explain the presence of the other two priests."

"In Issura, there is always an official inquiry when there has been a death on one of our ships," Luc said.

"And since I'm freshly ordained, Brother Luc is field training me," Jeremy added. "Though honestly, I wanted to see the inside of your manor. I've heard rumors of the decadence."

Both Luc and I glared at the young priest who shrugged. "Brother Kam says truth is always the best," he said in a sheepish tone.

Jeremy's addendum drew outright laughter from the ambassador. When he was able to calm himself, he called out, "Who was expecting a package from the Issuran captain?"

Silence reigned. Not even a whisper in the hall.

Quan leaned back in his chair, his gaze equally scanning his own people and his guests. "Now what could be so valuable or so dangerous that no one wants to claim their property?"

If the ambassador were attempting to fool us, he was doing an excellent job.

The Jing sorcerer rose, and for the first time I could see below his chest. The thing wrapped around his waist nearly made me choke on my bile. It was the hue of nothingness.

A section lifted a fraction. I felt its attention sweep the ensemble, then it fixated on me once it realized I was staring at it.

"This is surely an attempt by Issura to insult and embarrass your august personage, Your Excellency," the sorcerer said. His words would have been more menacing if they weren't the higher pitch of a eunuch's.

However, I took his abilities as well as his demon very seriously.

Despite my own fear, I took a step closer to the sorcerer and the demon. "Something has been puzzling me, Your Excellency. Why send such an important item via an Issuran ship instead of a Jing vessel?"

Quan followed my attention to his sorcerer. His fingers curled around the handle of his table knife. "Something I do not understand either, Lady Justice."

My gut said an internal matter of their nation was playing out. I was torn. Leaving would be prudent, but I feared letting a demon or one of their artifacts run loose in Orrin.

The sorcerer merely smiled at me. "So the rumors that you can see them are true."

The demon uncurled from its master's waist and leapt onto the table. Shouts of alarm rose from assemblage. Jing guards drew their weapons as did the concubine. She tried to insert herself between the sorcerer and Quan, but the ambassador shoved her back.

I didn't bother reaching for my sword when the demon launched itself at me. I knew from bitter experience steel couldn't harm it. Instead, I dropped to my back and used the demon's momentum and my boots to propel it over my head.

As I rolled to my feet, one of the guards tried to stab it with his spear.

Both the steel point and the wooden shaft shattered on impact. One swipe of the demon's clawed hand gutted the poor man.

It whirled and raced toward me again, but something was wrong. It didn't move like the ones I'd encountered last summer. It was slow in comparison. I easily evaded its rush.

"Kill the summoner!" I shouted. "Only way to banish it!"

Luc charged toward the dais, but Quan reacted first. He grabbed the collar of his sorcerer. With a flick of his wrist, he sliced open the man's throat.

I counted silently to myself as I dodged the demon's clumsy charges, but there was no pop of displaced air. No disappearance into its own dimension.

The demon paused, then barked, the low guttural sound that was their laughter. Laughing at us.

Horror engulfed me. Goddess help us. The sorcerer wasn't the thing's summoner.

The demon dived toward me, but a gesture from Luc drove it head first into the floor's marble tiles.

That same instant the concubine screamed. She dropped the long knife she'd drawn and clawed at her throat. Jeremy raced to her side.

Frigid fingers wrapped around my ankle, and the landing on polished stone knocked the wind out of me. A swift kick with my free leg didn't dislodge the demon. Ice formed inside my trapped boot.

I sucked in a deep breath past the pain. "Titus! Run!"

On my cue, he open the casket.

Everything in the room stopped.

The screaming. The panic. Even the casket hovered in mid-air.

Titus had done as I instructed. Open, drop, run. He was frozen half-way through his pivot for the main doors.

My spell had worked.

For the first time, I realized most of the diners had cleared out of the ambassador's great room. A handful in the doorway peered over their shoulder for one last look.

The remaining guards were all Jing. Crimson terror glowed from their visages, but they had stayed, which said a lot about the loyalty Quan inspired. No doubt they'd heard the stories of the demon wars. They definitely had seen what one could do to their fellow.

I reached down and pried the demon's talons from my ankle, wincing as the cold penetrated my gloves. Hopefully, there was no frostbite. The stinging in my toes reassured me that there was still some circulation. How long had the damned creature held onto Arturo before the captain had frozen to death?

Once I gained my feet, a few experimental steps cracked the thin layer of ice inside my boot. I limped over to the dais, sat down and emptied out the chips.

Luc was right. I needed a second half of a plan.

My next move required a little more thought. I stood and examined the room for what I could use.

Luc cupped something in his palm, his arm drawn back. I crossed to him and passed my hand over his. Active magic tingled through the leather. We'd need more than one light ball to eliminate the demon.

Over on the dais, Jeremy had managed to remove the jewel from the concubine, or more likely a body guard from her attempt to protect the ambassador. She slumped under the table. The skin at her throat glowed with raw flesh. Considering the amount of bright yellow blood, no major vessels were torn. She'd survive if I came up with a strategy.

Jeremy bent over the jewel where it rested on a plate. I peered closely at the jewel. Oddly, a thin layer of ash covered its surface. Again, magic tingled across my skin. I was a little relieved that Jeremy had devised a means to destroy the jewel.

Restarting time in this room would be necessary for Luc and Jeremy's abilities to work, but the demon wasn't going to lie still and let us kill it. So how to fix this?

I circled the demon. I couldn't coordinate with Luc and Jeremy if I stayed inside the temporal hole I'd created. But I wasn't sure I could extract myself without releasing the demon.

While killing whoever summoned the demon would be a far more acceptable resolution, I had a terrible feeling that person was thousands of leagues across the Peaceful Sea. I glanced at the jewel again. Something about it nagged me.

Focus. One problem at a time, Anthea.

The only certainty was to keep this room frozen in a single moment forever.

Until I died. Then my spell would fail, and the demon would be free to wreak havoc.

Movement at the edge of my vision drew my attention. One ebony claw slid inexorably across the dark blue tile to the lighter blue mortar. My heart threatened to choke me. It may take the demon years, but eventually it would reach the doorway.

I drew a deep breath and released it. The stakes were too high for me to fail this time.

Time appeared as threads around the edges of the room. Twisting, turning, weaving. And my spell had pushed a room-sized hole in that never-ending fabric. The threads weren't torn or cut. Simply shoved apart the way a needle slices through material. And I was the needle, which was start of the problem.

I crossed to where Jeremy was attempting to destroy the jewel and started tugging the strings back into place. Gently. One by one. Starting with ones behind me.

Once I had extracted myself, it was difficult to keep the hole intact. Sweat tickled my scalp, and I tightened my grip. Concentrated on each thread, verifying I wasn't letting go of the demon accidentally, before I released the string.

Behind me Jeremy gasped. A muffled feminine moan followed. Then the odor of rotten eggs.

"Brother, to me!" My body shook.

"Justice?" His robes rustled behind my right shoulder.

"Can you create more balls like the one in Brother Luc's hand, and keep them hovering by you until I tell you to release them at the demon?"

"How many?"

For the first time today, a bit of relief eased past the tension in my shoulders. "As many as you can, as powerful as you can, while I return Luc back into our time."

Both Titus and the ambassador would have be dealt with first since they were closer to me than Luc. I nudged more threads back into place.

The casket crashed to the floor. Titus took two steps before he realized the Jing guards were frozen where they stood. "Lady Justice?"

"Pick up the casket and put the jewel on the table in it without touching the damned thing."

"And me?" Quan said.

"Check the bleeding of your bodyguard's wound, Your Excellency." My voice wavered with the strain of holding back the time lines. "And keep the rest of your men out of my way."

I ignored the building heat of Jeremy's efforts behind me. Pushed the ambassador's instructions to the back of my awareness. Concentrated on separating Luc from the demon.

With a gasp, Luc jerked and jumped back from the prone figure on the floor. The tingle of his magic flared. "It worked?"

"Stop doubting me," I said through gritted teeth. "More balls before this thing escapes."

His silent chuckle at my poor choice of words tickled my mind, but he added to the growing volume of magic around us.

The strain of keeping the demon in a hole of time took its toll. My limbs shook. Sweat soaked my smallclothes. Dizziness swept my brain. The strands started to slip from my grasp.

"Now!" Time snapped back with my shout. Luc and Jeremy's magic converged on the demon.

It screamed. Not in pain or fear, but sheer unadulterated rage. It burned faster than Jing flash powder. Within a handful of heartbeats, nothing was left but a man-sized pile of cinders.

Luc caught me as my knees gave way.

"Wait!" Titus shouted. "No—"

We turned in time to see the concubine raise the casket. She brought it down on top of the jewel with a *crack*. The casket fell from her hands and bounced off the dais. When she wavered from her efforts, Quan wrapped his arms around her for support.

She looked at me. "This is not something you want to take back to your temple, Lady Justice."

I shrugged off Luc's hold and climbed onto the dais to take a closer look. The jewel lay shattered on the tabletop. There was no mistaking the tiny form among the shards. A baby demon. Dead and still.

"An egg." Luc's words were a harsh rumble behind me.

"And it stayed here because it was laid in this dimension?" I wrapped my arms around my body, staving off the shivers that threatened.

"That would be my guess." He straightened and rubbed his chin. "This doesn't bode well. If these . . . eggs are stockpiled somewhere—"

"Whoever has them," Titus interjected, "is doling them out. Otherwise, we'd have been overrun by demons before now."

"It . . . explains much," Quan's bodyguard whispered.

The ambassador glanced at her before he faced me. "It would be best if this was not spoken of outside my chambers until it can be rectified at home." His grim tone promised fire and pain.

"I understand your position, Your Excellency, but I have duties to my people as well." I paused for a moment before I added, "Would a day be sufficient?"

He nodded. "More than enough."

Once outside of the mansion, all four men insisted I return to my temple for rest.

I started to argue, but wave of dizziness nearly threw me to the cobble-stones. I had to grab my horse for support. "Maybe you're right."

Luc laughed. "For once, I have another priest to confirm your admis-sion."

I made an obscene gesture in response. More embarrassment followed when I needed Little Bear's assistance mounting.

Luc patted my horse's neck. "I'll inform Magistrate DiCook and Duke Marco of the status of this case." *I'll visit later tonight.*

Warmth filled me at his silent statement, but I kept to the immediate matter. "Tell His Grace to instruct his ship masters not to accept any last moment packages from Jing."

"Of course, Justice."

I turned my horse, only to have Titus lay a hand on the reins.

"M'lady . . ." His coloring turned brilliant yellow as he realized what he'd done and jerked his hand back. He stared up at me. "I beg forgiveness. I just wanted—" There was an audible gulp. "I wanted to thank you for discovering the truth about Captain Arturo."

Except we didn't know the truth. Had the captain been complicit in smuggling the egg into Issura? Or was he an innocent dupe? Either way, he'd paid with his life.

None of which Titus needed to hear. I inclined my head. "Please tell his kin that if his last declaration isn't on file with the Temple of Death, to deliver it to my clerk in the morning. Given the circumstances, I'll do what I can to expedite the process."

"Many thanks, m'lady." He stepped back, and Little Bear and I made our weary way home.

A long nap, and lots of tea, restored me. Later that night, I was relatively coherent as I stamped out my own report to the Reverend Mother concerning the day's incident.

I still questioned why the Jing sorcerer had given Quan's female companion the egg. In my head, I could hear the Reverend Mother's querulous reply. *Not our business as long as both demons are dead.*

A crash from the kitchen jerked my hand. I dropped the metal tiles and raced for the rear of the temple. Little Bear and the rest of the wardens ran in my wake.

My entrance was halted by the bright white-yellow light of the room. I lifted my hand to shield my eyes from glare of the ovens and cook fire. The bizarre sight of my elderly, sweet-natured cook, holding a strange woman at bay with a butcher knife in one hand and a fish scaler in the other left me speechless.

"I caight this Jing wench sneaking through mah kitchen, m'lady." Deborah shook her butcher knife at the intruder to emphasize her point.

The woman bowed from her waist, empty hands outstretched. "Forgive me for the intrusion, Justice. After today's events, it was deemed prudent to speak to you privately without the news of this meeting spread further than either of us would care."

I blinked and tried to hide my surprise. The voice was that of Ambassador Quan's concubine. Instead of the miniscule slip of silk from earlier, she wore the plain leggings and tunic of the temples.

"Forgive me as well. We were not formally introduced this afternoon."

"I am Shi Hua, a priestess of Light."

I gave up on shielding my emotions, confusion being paramount. Now I knew why the sorcerer had targeted her, but it also opened numerous other questions. "A most unexpected pleasure, Sister."

"May we speak alone?" she asked again.

"Of course." I inclined my head. "I'm having my evening tea. Would you care to join me?" Fortunately, Deborah took my hint and lowered her knives.

Shi Hua bowed again. "I would be honored."

I led her to the very same receiving room where I'd started the morning. Once the sister was seated and the tea arrived, I dismissed Little Bear. He glowered. I stared right back. He finally stomped out of the room and slammed the door for good measure.

"I seem to have upset him," Shi Hua remarked as she accepted a steaming cup from me.

"Actually, I have. He's throwing a tantrum because he missed the entertainment in the ambassador's great room this afternoon." I took a sip from my own cup. "To what do I owe the honor of a visit from a hidden priestess?"

She set aside her tea. "I am sure you have surmised I am not the ambassador's consort."

I nodded and waved for her to continue.

"Not only do Ambassador Quan and I owe you our lives, the emperor of Jing owes you a great debt as well. We had assumed the recent infiltration of Issuran nobility by demons was an isolated incident."

She stared at the sculpture of Balance and her next words were hard, nothing like her previous dulcet tones. "The Imperial guard and our own wardens raided the School of Sorcery a few hours ago. Until you, until today, we had no idea the masters' sashes were—" A shudder racked her. "My Reverend Father said there hadn't been such a demon battle since the end of the wars."

"Surely, your Temple of Balance received the incident report from the Reverend Mother of Issura. Why did they doubt—"

She faced me again. "Because human survival depended on our unity against the demons for a thousand years. Now, our nations bicker between themselves. Our own Reverend Father of Conflict counseled that your temple's dispatch was a ploy."

Why was she telling me this? Then it hit me. She wasn't just the ambassador's bodyguard. She was a spy as well.

I choose a more appropriate phrase. "You're a distance-speaker. The reason the ambassador's sorcerer gave you the jewel was to take out a potential threat to him and his pet by alerting your temple."

"Yes, and the School feared you would inevitably learn their secret. You were targeted next, according to my Reverend Father." Shi Hua poured herself more to tea. She clutched the fine ceramic from her homeland as if it were a lifeline. "They found the cache of eggs that were laid here during the end of the last invasion."

I tapped my forefinger against my lips. "That's why the one today did not move as fast as the ones I encountered last summer. It wasn't summoned. It was hatched here."

She nodded. There was a long silence before she blurted, "You are able to see the demons. Can you teach us?"

"I'm sorry—"

"The emperor will pay any price!"

I set aside my cup and leaned forward. "My vision is an accident, Sister." I told her my tale. Of my arrogant assumption that I could do what the healers couldn't. Of my lack of reference concerning the sense of sight when I developed the spell. Of my belief I could escape servitude to the Temple of Balance if I was no longer blind.

"A pity," she whispered.

"That I didn't escape the temple?"

"That your gift can't be spread."

I reached for her cup and gently set it on the table before I took her chilled hands between mine. "Sister, I can't see the shift of shades in a sunrise or sunset. All I know of flowers is the soft touch of their petals and their fragrance. I will never be able to see a rainbow except through someone else's eyes."

"But—"

"The best thing we can do is share information. All of it. Two demon appearances after a century of quiet?" I released her and leaned back. "I don't believe in coincidences."

"Neither do I."

We both rose and clasped hands.

I escorted her to the rear yard, Little Bear trailing behind us. She easily scaled the wall and disappeared over the stable roof of the inn across the rear alley. I wondered if she had sensed the same presence in the temple garden that I did.

"I'll be meditating by the fountain if you need me."

Little Bear reached out for me, but brought himself short. He still forgot I could see, even if my vision wasn't normal. "But, Justice, what about your safety?"

"I doubt we have another visitor from Jing tonight." I turned for the garden.

Little Bear hesitated a moment for he called out to chastise the two wardens on midnight duty for not stopping the intruder. I smiled to myself. I suspected he hadn't left the doors to the receiving room the entire time Shi Hua was there. He would be even more cross if he knew the wardens had missed the second visitor.

I walked along the outer path when a strong arm pulled me behind a tree. Familiarity made me sink into Luc's hold.

What do you think? I asked when he ended his kiss. We didn't dare speak aloud. The ramifications if my wardens caught us in a compromising position would be worse than a foreign priestess penetrating temple security.

Do you have any idea how unnerving it is seeing through your eyes?

I'm more concerned about what you think about Shi Hua's story.

He glanced at the night sky. *You're not going to want to hear it.*

I drew back. *If Issura is in danger—*

He looked down at me. *Despite your determination to fail and your surly nature, you're developing a knack for diplomacy.*

I made a fisted and punched his bicep. *Get out of here before Little Bear finds you.*

After one last kiss, he scrambled up the tree and over the wall. Shi Hua's stunt would call an end to our late night trysts.

But his parting words made me question my life as I settled near the fountain to meditate. My adolescent effort to avoid fate and responsibility had inadvertently saved thousands of lives in less than a year. Maybe temple life truly was where the Goddess meant for me to be.

But I would still fight Her every step of the way.

The same way I'd fight the demons.

**Turn the page for a sneak preview of Justice Anthea
and Brother Luc's first full-length adventure,
*A Question of Balance.***

A Question of Balance

Excerpt © 2016, Suzan Harden

Since it was Rest Day, I was still in my bedclothes and breaking my fast when Duke Marco's messenger arrived. Setting aside the rich cinnamon bread, I glared at both the nervous young man and my personal assistant Sivan. "Tell me, is there a chance His Grace, his lady wife or his retainers might let me finish one morning meal in peace?"

"When the stars fall from the skies, Justice?" Humor edged Sivan's response.

My displeasure settled on the messenger. His bright scarlet face and hands quivered.

I smiled sweetly, but the boy wasn't comforted by my demeanor. My appearance discomfited nearly everyone the first time they saw me, my lover being the sole exception. "What is so important that your master could not wait for a reasonable time, like *after* Second Morning?"

"My apologies, L-Lady Justice. Duke Marco respectfully requests your presence. A-a body was found in one of the keep's wine barrels." His voice cracked on the last syllable.

Orrin was the third largest city in Issura and had the second largest seaport. While crime wasn't rampant, the city's main problem was disorderly conduct from sailors on shore leave. Or it was until I was assigned as the resident justice last summer. Even then, I was rarely called to investigate normal offenses like theft or smuggling, which the Orrin magistrate and his peacekeepers handled quite ably. It was for inconvenient things like this.

I shoved my plate away, wiped my mouth with my napkin and stood. "Thank you so very much for destroying my appetite."

The boy whimpered. From his voice and his manner, he was the highest ranking page available. No matter if he had heard the rumors many times over, my red eyes had made more than a few grown men wet their small-clothes.

"Run across the street, and request a priest from Light to accompany me."

"Y-yes, ma'am." He fled as if I'd summon demons to eat his scrawny hide.

Sivan didn't bother to hide her laughter any longer.

"You did that on purpose," I accused. According to the gossip I overhead on my way to the temple kitchen one evening, my nickname was the Red Justice. So far, no one had the effrontery to call me that to my face.

Sivan folded her hands primly in front of her. "He said he was instructed to only deliver the message to you, m'lady. Far be it for me to interfere with his duty."

I stalked over to the wardrobe in the corner of my private chamber. Inside were several sets of formal cloaks. To any one else, they looked identical, the black of the Temple of Balance from hood to ankle. But for me, I could still see the blood stains on all of them.

Various laundresses' best efforts not withstanding.

Out of some sense of perversity, I chose the set that still carried the stains of the sorcerer Samael, a distant member of the royal family whom I'd illegally executed to save Duke Marco.

And the world.

Once I'd donned leggings, boots and a silk undershirt, I tied on my robes, pulled up the hood, and added my sword to the ensemble. In the half year since Marco's parents had been found guilty of treason due to their conspiracy with Samael DiRoy, little incidents had been occurring. Small challenges to the duke's authority. Carefully crafted insults.

It didn't help that he'd married a commoner who'd been conceived during the Spring Rituals, though the Lady Katarina was a healer of no mean skill.

So far, the young man had been holding his own. But a body found on his estate would only escalate the problems with the nobility, even if the young lord and his retinue were innocent. Nothing like a good scandal to stir the masses.

I reached the stables to find High Brother Luc, chief priest of Orrin's Temple of Light, already mounted, waiting for me with two of his wardens. Cold raindrops trickled dark purple tracks down his cloak.

I had to hide my delight that he came. "Brother, please don't bother on such an ugly day. Either of your junior priests would do in this circumstance. Surely as the head of your temple, you have more important duties."

"Considering where the body was found, it seemed that our best truthspeller should accompany you, Justice." Amusement flavored his tone. Now that we were both permanently assigned to Orrin, we went through this dance of words every time we met in public since we could not often meet privately without arousing suspicions.

By the Twelve, I missed sleeping with him.

I inclined my head. "Thank you for your assistance, Brother."

Little Bear, one of my own wardens, moved to assist me on my horse. I glared at him, my foul mood spilling over once again.

Luc muffled his laugh, and the warden had the grace to say sheepishly, "My apologies, Justice. I forgot."

Reining in my temper, I said, "I understand, but this behavior must stop."

"Before she knocks someone's teeth out," Luc added. Like Sivan earlier, he didn't bother hiding his laughter.

"Yes, m'lady." Little Bear bowed and turned to his own horse.

It was habit on the warden's part, I knew. Every priestess in my order was blind.

Every single one except me.

The wardens and clerks acted as the justice's eyes. None of the staff at Orrin knew what to do with a sighted justice. Not that I saw the world as they saw it, but I had vision enough I wasn't helpless by any means.

I climbed on my precious Nassa and patted her neck. "Shall we discover what's troubling Duke DiMara today?"

Luc snorted. "I'd say it was his ruined wine."

I couldn't be angry with the page for spreading unnecessary gossip. Luc could charm the knowledge out of anyone without the need of a truthspell.

We guided our mounts through the postern gate, down the alley that separated my goddess's temple from that of Mother, and up Temple Street, the main thoroughfare of the city. The business district gave way to small shops and eateries. Orrin was rich enough that the streets were cobblestoned, but the winter rains kept most of the citizens indoors despite the absence of mud.

Small homes appeared between the merchant buildings. Gradually the shops disappeared, and the houses grew larger as we climbed the bluffs on the north side of the bay.

The DiMara estate overlooked the city and harbor, an imposing stone enclave that still bore signs of its original purpose as a fortress. A guardsman swung open the ornate wrought iron gate, a show of the family's wealth, as we approached. The duke's family controlled a majority of the Orrin harbor trade, and those ships they didn't own outright, they had invested in over the years.

Two stableboys took our horses while the guardsman led us on foot to a warehouse on the left. The dry interior was welcome after our short, wet ride.

Orrin's magistrate, Malven DiCook, was not.

"'Bout time his lordship's pet priestess got here." He coughed and spat on the floor, close enough to me to be thoroughly disgusting but intentionally missing my boot. Duke Marco wasn't the only one dealing with insults and challenges to authority, but the ones aimed at me weren't so carefully crafted.

If I had the evidence Malven was involved in the former lord and lady's treason, I'd behead the bastard without blinking. But I didn't, which meant I had to tread lightly around the duly elected city magistrate.

And tolerate the sickly sweet odor of the damn licorice-scented dye he used to disguise the effects of age in his hair and beard.

He hooked his thumbs in his belt and rocked back on his heels. "His lordship wouldn't let me examine the body until you arrived."

I brushed back the hood of my cloak and stepped closer. Being a tall woman was handy at times. I met the magistrate's glare before he turned his attention toward the floor. Sometimes, my idiotic attempt to give myself sight came in handy for unnerving my antagonist.

He muttered the Cantish word for "freak."

"No," I answered in the same language. "I was chosen by the Goddess. If you have an issue with her selection, I'm sure the Reverend Mother could arrange an audience for you." I didn't add my personal opinion of his hygiene habits.

He jerked and shuffled a step backward. I didn't know whether it was due to my knowledge of Cantish or my not-so-subtle threat. Nor did I wish to probe his thoughts to find out. Mucking out Duke Marco's horse stalls would be a far more pleasant task.

Luc's amusement at the magistrate's reaction tickled my mind, but he said nothing.

"This way m'lady." The guardsman beckoned us to follow. He marched for the opening that yawned in the floor of the storage room.

Luc faced our wardens. "Two up. Two down with us." Without a word, one of his and Little Bear moved to positions where they could watch both the main door, the passage to the underground storage rooms, and each other's backs.

Marco's guardsman lit an oil lamp and led our retinue and the magistrate down the wide wooden ramp. The air was terribly dry for such a miserable, wet day. Small bowls sat in alcoves along the wall. The bone salt in them absorbed the moisture in the air to prevent mold and rot.

At the bottom of the ramp, my desiccated airways itched from both the mineral and the sawdust coating the floor. Despite the sweet scent of mountain pine, another sickly smell met me. The guardsman gestured to the wide double doorway to our right.

I strode past the guardsmen to find Duke Marco, his wife and sister, his steward, and another household servant on one side. Facing them were three of the city's peacekeepers. A wine barrel stood upright between the two sets of observers. The tension in the wine room was more suffocating than the odor of death.

"You and your household seem rather intent on disturbing my morning meals, Your Grace." I nodded to the women. "Lady Katarina, Lady Alessa."

"Truly, I would prefer not to." Marco's grim humor matched mine. "However, the circumstances warranted your curious mind."

"Would it make you more comfortable if I provided you a knife to threaten someone with, Justice Anthea?" Lady Katarina offered with the same amusement as her husband. She rested a bright red hand over her prominent stomach.

Sometimes, the odd eyesight I'd given myself let me see things that others couldn't. Like the rise in the lady's body temperature. Knowing she was with child before she did had been entertaining.

An odd sort of friendship had sprung between Lady Katarina and myself over the last six months. Probably because we were both products of the Temple of Love's Spring Rituals. Definitely because I had saved her and her husband's lives from his deranged mother and the demons her pet sorcerer had summoned.

"That will be unnecessary, m'lady," I replied and brushed the pommel of my sword at my shoulder. "I've learned to carry bigger weapons when you two are involved."

"If you're going to do nothing but joke with His Grace, maybe you should leave." The magistrate's irritation felt like steel scraped across slate.

I turned my gaze on DiCook. "I didn't realize you had been named the Reverend Mother of Balance."

"Your predecessor had a sense of decorum in these matters," he shot back.

Sometimes, I wondered if the elderly justice who held the temple seat here before me was willfully, as well as literally blind. But that wasn't fair. None of the priest or priestesses of the eleven other temples detected so much as a whiff of trouble with Marco's parents before it was too late.

Unless I'd totally misread their allegiances.

I had gotten lucky, and I knew it. Otherwise, we'd be neck-deep in another demon war now.

"Really, Sir Magistrate? In reviewing her records, I did not come across any accounts of bodies in wine barrels. Care to enlighten me?"

He muttered another obscenity under his breath, but otherwise remained silent.

The duke and his party wisely said nothing as well while I crossed to the source of the odor and peered inside. I couldn't distinguish much in the deep green mass because the body had cooled to the same temperature as liquid it floated in, so I inhaled deeply.

I looked up at Luc who had joined me. "He or she didn't loose their bowels in there."

"She," he corrected. At my quizzical expression, he added, "Too much hair floating at the top of the barrel."

"Could be Pagonian." I shrugged. Both men and women of Issura's neighbor to the north only cut their locks during a period of family grieving.

Luc shook his head. "No. Hair's too pale even soaked in dark red wine."

I sighed. "I suppose I should examine the timeline before we pull whoever it is out of the barrel."

Luc grunted and looked over his shoulder. "Duke Marco, when was this barrel brought onto your estate?"

The nobleman's sister Alessa was the one who answered. "Three days ago, High Brother."

"Was the wine seal intact?" I asked.

The three nobles looked at the steward who turned to the man beside him who nervously shuffled his feet before he answered. "The wax weren't broken, m'lady, but the winery stamp weren't there neither." He shrugged. "We git 'em that way sometimes, usually in the summer. The tops melt."

"But this is the middle of winter," I said softly.

"During winter cleaning, the lads at the winery set the barrels outside in the sun," the steward volunteered. "The air temperature is cold enough to keep the wine fresh, but the direct light softens the wax."

"Sounds reasonable," Luc said.

Luc turned back to me. *We can always confirm with the priests at Vintner.* Out loud, he said, "With her being dead, I won't be able to track her."

I grinned at him. "Afraid the Wilding priests might show you up?"

DiCook stomped over to the barrel. "If you two are finished making light of someone's murder, maybe you'll get around to finding the culprit."

"Murder? Who said anything about murder?" I couldn't resist needling the magistrate.

His face turned a brilliant scarlet. "So this poor woman decided to take a swim in a barrel of his lordship's wine?"

"We cannot assume anything at this point." My Luc, ever the voice of reason. "What do you need, Anthea?" His question was for the benefit of everyone else in the room.

"Just some quiet," I murmured. I pulled off my gloves and settled cross-legged on the cold flagstone floor. With one hand on the barrel and one on a shard of decorative onyx embedded next to the slate, I concentrated.

The stone quivered beneath my palm, eager to tell its story. It paid more attention to the vagaries of the mobile beings than its slate brothers.

I tugged the strings of time with the stone's assistance, unwinding back to four days ago. Luc and the rest would see transparent figures moving faster than usual. I could only see gray ghosts drifting around and through the colored figures of the living in the storage room. Two phantom men rolled a barrel out of the room.

"Hold." Luc's baritone rumbled through the air.

I paused the release of the time thread.

"Names," he demanded.

"That's William and me," squeaked the retainer standing with the steward.

"Name," Luc snapped.

"Bartholomew, m'lord," the retainer squeaked again.

"I told them to bring up a barrel of the local rose for dinner the night before the delivery," the steward offered.

"Luc," I said through gritted teeth.

"My apologies. Continue." At least he actually sounded sorry, but I don't think he truly understood the strain of what I was doing.

I let the string of time the onyx showed me slide forward. Several ghostly men rolled barrels down the ramp.

"Who are the three with Bartholomew?" Luc asked.

"The man on the barrel with him is Julian, one of the Duke's retainers," the steward answered. "The other two are the vineyard's transporters."

"Do you know them?"

The steward shook his head. "Rubio and his son normally bring the Orrin shipments. These two said Rubio had hurt his back, and they'd been hired to deliver the barrels."

"Names," Luc snapped again.

"Th-they didn't give their names." A green sheen of sweat appeared at the steward's hairline. "Their paperwork had the vineyard's seal."

Luc folded his arms. "Where did the shipment come from?"

"The Pana Valley," Lady Alessa and the steward answered at the same time.

"Lord Aleister DiGrove's estate," the duke's sister added.

Luc's concern matched my own. If this turned out to be a power play within the nobility, things could turn very ugly very fast.

I let the rest of the timeline slide through my grip. But once the barrel in question was stored, it remained in place until Bartholomew and the man he named as William tapped it this morning.

"Well, that wasn't a damn bit helpful," Luc murmured.

I thanked the onyx before I shook the feeling back into my fingers and rose to my feet. "Let's drain the barrel and get her out."

"Shame about the wine." Luc stepped out of the way.

I could hear DiCook's teeth grind, but he kept silent.

The steward and Bartholomew set buckets under the tap to drain the ruined red while the guardsman went off to fetch an old blanket. Once a sufficient amount had been removed that we wouldn't flood the cellar if we accidentally tipped it, Luc and I peered in the barrel once more.

I pulled my gloves back on. "Ready?"

"We can do it if her ladyship can't."

I didn't have to look at DiCook to hear the sneer in his voice. "My thanks, Magistrate, but I can't have you or your men vomit on the body and contaminate it." I hooked my arm under one of the corpse's shoulders. "Ready"

Luc grabbed the other shoulder. Together, Luc and I lifted the deceased out of the barrel. She was heavier than she should have been, her skin having absorbed a great deal of wine. On the shores of the Peaceful Sea, one couldn't help seeing their share of drowning victims. We carefully settled the nude body on the blanket.

I brushed the soaked locks away from the face. A sharp gasp came from Lady Katarina. I looked at noblewoman. "You recognize her?"

She stepped closer. "The face is distorted but—" She gave a sharp nod. "Sister Gretchen from the Temple of Love. She was my playmate when we were children."

I could feel Luc watching me, which was understandable. For the six months since my assignment to Orrin, I'd managed to avoid the chief priestess of the Temple of Love, but I couldn't any longer.

With one of her people dead, I was going to have to face my mother.

Acknowledgments

First of all, thanks to Elisabeth Waters who bought the first two Justice short stories for *Marion Zimmer Bradley's Sword and Sorceress* anthology series.

Next round of appreciation goes to Nicola Seaton-Clark, who produced the audio version of "Justice" for the Far-Fetched Fables podcast, and voice artist Deanna Sanchez, who brought Justice Anthea to life. The podcast is still available at Far-Fetched Fables No. 38.

Finally, many thanks to all the readers who said they wanted more.

About the Author

Suzan Harden is a recovering attorney who writes fiction to regain her sanity. She currently lives in the Great Lakes region with a husband who believes writing is a practical career option and a kid who thinks she's too enamored with zombies.

For more information or to be added to her mailing list, visit Suzan's website at www.suzanharden.com